RED ALERT: MISSILES INBOUND

Creative Texts Publishers products are available at special discounts for bulk purchase for sale promotions, premiums, fund-raising, and educational needs. For details, write Creative Texts Publishers, PO Box 50, Barto, PA 19504, or visit www.creativetexts.com

RED ALERT: MISSILES INBOUND
Book One of The Oort Chronicles
Published by Creative Texts Publishers
PO Box 50
Barto, PA 19504
www.creativetexts.com

ISBN: 978-0-578-49730-3

RED ALERT: MISSILES INBOUND

BY CLIFF DEANE

CREATIVE TEXTS PUBLISHERS
Barto, Pennsylvania

This book is dedicated to Mrs. Eileen Nearing Greene,
a dear friend of more than fifty years.

It is estimated that as many as two-trillion comets still reside in the Oort Cloud, which is the farthest known limit of our Solar System.

CONTENTS

THE SCIENCE STUFF

The Oort Cloud

The Star System named Sol

It is estimated that as many as two-trillion comets still reside in the Oort Cloud, which is the farthest known limit of our Solar System.

The distance is so great that a number written in miles would have absolutely no meaning, even to Astronomers. To create a measurable distance, Scientists now use a term called the AU (Astronomical Unit). One AU is equal to the distance from the Earth to the Sun, some ninety-three million miles. In math notation that would be 93,000,000, and since the Oort Cloud measures out to as much as ten-thousand AUs, using the number nine-hundred and thirty billion miles becomes incomprehensible.

The Holly Thorne Comet began its descent toward the Sun after being struck by, and fused with, several other dirty snowballs. These collisions sent the now huge comet tumbling out of the Oort. As she began falling toward Sol, Holly Thorne picked up other small comets. She now measured thirty miles across. The series of glancing blows created a wobbling rotation.

The voyage of Holly would take two-thousand three-hundred, and fifty-nine years from the time it began to plummet toward Sol. The birth of Jesus Christ was still three-hundred and fifty years in the Earth's future.

CHAPTER ONE

The Discovery

MT. PALOMAR OBSERVATORY
PALOMAR, CALIFORNIA

Trent Allison sat at his desk looking over computer images of the night sky, searching for anomalies that portrayed objects moving through the heavens that did not follow the normal path.

"Hey, little guy, just where are you going in such a hurry?" asked Trent of one such anomaly. He directed the computer to take the available data on this, as yet, unnamed comet, and extrapolate a possible trajectory. The data returned by the computer caused Trent to run the information twice more. The results were the same; this could be a close rendezvous. He garnered his findings, then called his Supervisor, Doug Shelton, to ask for a few moments to discuss his discovery.

"Sure thing, Trent, I'm taking my lunch break. Why don't you come on down now, if that works for you?"

"Yes, sir, I'll be there in five minutes with my own lunch. I'm transferring my data to your desktop, now."

"Good deal, I'll see you in five." Doug pushed the button that ended the call before turning to his desktop computer.

Trent rarely hurried anywhere, but he made an exception for his new discovery. He knocked on Doug's Office Door and heard his boss say, "Come on in, Trent."

Trent entered the office and took the seat offered by Doug, who said, "Well, doesn't this just suck? When did you first come across this potential harbinger of bad news?"

"About an hour ago; I was running overlays of the last thirty days along the Jupiter quadrant when this little guy showed up. I ran a projected trajectory, and my computer says it may pass us, but if it does, its passage will be between the Earth and Moon."

"Did I hear you right, *may* pass us? Now, isn't that definitive? Okay, what does your computer say about the chances of it slamming into us?" asked Doug.

"Doug, I don't want to be Chicken Little, but my station says between an 85 and 92% with a plus or minus 4% chance of it making an impact. Sir, I need to run my raw data through the Big Bertha computer. Doug, if I didn't think this Comet could prove to be a potential strike threat, I wouldn't ask, but we need Bertha's deep computations."

Doug looked over his reading glasses at Trent and asked, "How far out is she?"

"According to my station she is nearly eight-hundred million miles out and moving at close to forty-five thousand miles per hour, so, my estimate is around two years out."

"Yeah, I agree, but the scheduled users are gonna be so mad that their breath intake could suck a golf ball through a garden hose. Some of these guys have been waiting for two years to have some of Bertha's time, but you're right. Okay, you have her for forty-eight hours. I'll get with the Jet Propulsion Lab to give them a heads-up on her. We'll give them what we have now, and they can also run it through their big computers. Oh, have you checked to see if you are the first to see our visitor?"

Now Trent's face lit up with a smile resembling Alice's Cheshire Cat and with eyes bright with joy said, "Yes, sir, I did. Apparently, I am the first."

Doug rose from his chair and reached across the desk to shake Trent's hand. "Well, my friend, good for you, well done. Being the first means you get to name it. Have you thought of a good moniker?"

"Yes, sir, I have," grinned Trent. "I have decided to name her after my ex-wife, Holley Thorne."

Doug was a bit surprised and said, "Damn Trent, that's quite an honor for her, and, I might add, a very thoughtful thing for you to do."

Trent's smile only grew as he added, "I decided to name it after Holley because she is such a cold, miserable, whining, and complaining harpy who has made me want to stick my head in a gas oven many times."

Doug and Trent both laughed loud and hard. "Good one, Trent, but what will you really name it?"

Trent stopped laughing and said, "Holley Thorne."

Immediately after Trent's meeting with Doug, the word went out that a new, fast-moving object, probably a Comet named Holley Thorne was rapidly making its way toward the Sun.

NASA quickly rearranged the most advanced orbital telescope, Hubble V, rotating around the Red Sands Mars Colony to update the track of Holley Thorne. Once word of Holley Thorne got out, everyone at Red Sands was disappointed that they would miss out on the fireworks since they were not in the path of Holley's Tail.

Trent spent the next two days in Big Bertha's Lab fine-tuning his data and was somewhat relieved when she spat out a best guess trajectory that indicated Holley would miss the Earth by nearly two-hundred thousand miles on March 6, two years hence in 2118. Two-hundred thousand miles in the vastness of space was a distance which was described as being smaller than the width of the head of a needle, and according to Bertha, the odds of a collision was still in the 45% range.

Bertha also pointed out that Earth would quickly pass through Holley's tail which stretched out behind her for nearly two-hundred million miles. Holley Thorne is thirty miles wide, twice the size of the McNaught Comet which passed the Earth in 2007.

Trent was thrilled to learn of Earth's passage through Holley's tail, and he thought that the Comet's tail of two-hundred million miles was about right for his ex. He quickly realized that the light show would be even more spectacular than the Comet which buzzed the Earth a couple of hundred years ago. He thought that comet had flashed by sometime around 1918, just after the end of World War I, and just before the Spanish Flu Pandemic (H1N1) of that same year which killed as many as one hundred million people worldwide.

729 Days to Holley Thorne

MARCH 7, 2116, AD
PRESIDENTIAL CONFERENCE ROOM
WHITE HOUSE

President Eileen N. Greene convened her National Security Council to discuss the Holley Thorne Comet's potential danger to the Earth. One by one the President met each member's eyes, gauging their concern. "Ladies and Gentlemen, I sincerely hope your whiz kids have come up with a way to move this comet to well outside the orbit of Luna. NASA, let's start with you."

"Yes, Madame President," said Gordon Winters the NASA Chief, "Fortunately we do have a two-year window, and we are able to use several Asteroid Mining Vessels for this mission. They are currently at Red Sands dropping off cargo and taking on provisions now.

"There are, however, two potential hiccups. First, as this is the first ever attempt to move a stellar body by half a million miles, two years may not prove a sufficient window to move Holley Thorne outside the orbit of the moon. We just don't know for sure. All of our computer simulations say yes, but ultimately this mission is in its infancy. If the safety factor presents a significant possibility of directing the comet into a collision with Luna, well, we must think long and hard. Yet, with a projected clearance of only forty-thousand miles from the moon, the odds of a strike are already very high, our computers estimate a 50% chance of a hit.

"The second concern is that the debris field from a melting comet creates an extremely hazardous mission for the ships and crews of the vessels assigned to push it outside of the moon's orbit. There are many huge rocks in that tail traveling at forty-five thousand miles per hour. Now, having said all this, I can tell you that we can launch the ships within thirty-six hours. Three of them are currently being provisioned and equipped as we speak."

"I see," said the President, "I think I understand the risks involved, but can't we just launch some nukes to blow the damned thing to hell?"

Winters said, "Madame President, this comet is the largest ever recorded. It is roughly thirty miles across. Holley Thorne is twice the size of Comet McNaught, which was *previously* the largest comet ever recorded. Attempting to blow it to hell could well be problematic, in that we would likely just break Holley up into Mount Everest sized chunks that would most likely change the trajectory, causing strikes both on the moon and the Earth, and If that happens, well, we will go the way of the dinosaurs.

"Ma'am, I am afraid that the nuclear option is, unfortunately, not a viable response to Holley Thorne. Though dangerous, I believe that we must try to push it outside the orbit of the moon."

Mack Holland, Chief of Homeland Security interrupted saying, "If Holley is that big, won't she weigh too much to just push around?"

Gordon swallowed his smile before answering, "Mack, don't forget that in the vacuum of outer space, there is no element of weight."

Eileen asked how the comet would be nudged.

"The ships are equipped with stand-off lasers which will fire short bursts into the left side of Holley. The heat they generate will cause the ice to boil and act as jet propulsion. This will create sufficient force to slowly alter her trajectory. Asteroid mining vessels use them in their normal day to day operations.

"Madame President we can launch by 9 March. The ships will intercept the comet in roughly six months by launching from Mars. Our vessels can readily match the speed of the comet, and the mission will take roughly ten to fourteen months to push Holley outside the orbit of the moon.

"There is, however, one thing of which I am absolutely certain; the mining crews are going to make some very heavy demands, considering the personal risk involved. Be prepared to agree to whatever they want. We have no time for negotiating, and ultimately, they hold all the cards."

Eileen asked, "Gordon, why are we using civilian mining vessels? Isn't this something NASA or our Space Defense Force (SDF) should be handling?"

"No, ma'am, the reason we must use the mining vessels is that their ships have both enhanced, and stand-off armored plating. Such armor is absolutely necessary for them, as the asteroid belt is a regular shooting gallery. Our ships don't have this armor because of the age-old bug-a-boo called budget constraints."

"I see," said Eileen, "well, that is a problem for another time. All right, Gordon, get them launched and let's put an end to this threat. I can see that my next hurdle will be to keep Russia, China, and India from using nukes. Those folks still think that if one nuke won't do the job, then use ten. Yes, when you think like a hammer, everything looks like a nail."

"Madame President," said Dr. Tyler Deen, a virologist, and the CDC Director, "there remains another consideration."

The President looked warily at Deen before saying, "Yes, Dr. and that would be what?"

"Madame President, we have learned that comets often carry the elements necessary for life, to include viruses. I don't wish to raise a panic here, but we must devise a failsafe to ensure that these ships do not return to Earth, or Mars until we can be assured that they carry no threat, significantly that of viral contamination."

"Yes, I suppose that would be the prudent thing to do. Admiral Perry, I would like for you to work with your Computer Gurus and come up with a computer virus that, upon command will not allow the ships to attain orbit should they become infected by, oh, anything."

"Yes, ma'am, I'll get right on it."

"You know, for the very first time in my life, I kind of wish the old United Nations hadn't fallen completely apart after we withdrew from it back in 2022," said President Greene.

The President then spoke with each remaining member of her staff and, finding no better alternatives, set the launch in motion.

CHAPTER TWO

MARCH 7, 2116, AD

HEINLEIN SPACE PORT

RED SANDS, MARS COLONY

Reginald (Reg) Lee, the Space Port Administrator at the Red Sands facility, ended his call from Gordon Winters. Gordon was the Earthside NASA Boss.

Reg stood 5'8" in height, with brown eyes and deep black hair. Though he was of Taiwanese ancestry, the place of his birth was at the Mars, Red Sands Colony. Reg loved Mars and the only time spent on Earth had been for his Collegiate education at Cal Tech. Besides the fact that Earth caused him to weigh nearly three times more than on Mars, the danged place was green, with a blue sky. No, Reg definitely preferred the red tones of Mars.

The colony existed under a huge series of domes, connected by tubes, both above and below the surface and were constantly being expanded to accommodate the growth of the Mars Colony.

The planet was being terraformed, needing another two- hundred years to complete the process. Reg was glad that he wouldn't be around to see the beauty of Mars turn blue and green.

By 2100 AD, human life expectancy was well beyond a hundred years. By 2120 AD, the estimation of the normal human lifespan was poised to take another exponential leap in longevity through both medical procedures and bionic hardware. These new technologies would modify the gene structure retarding the aging process, as well as the introduction of an individual Artificial Intelligence, inserted directly into the cerebellum of the brain. This device was the size of a grain of rice.

Reg had the sole responsibility of ensuring the orbiting freighters assigned to the Holley Thorne mission were resupplied and prepped for launch within the next twenty-four hours.

Using his intercom, he asked his secretary to find Jim Bream and ask him to drop by. Jim was the perfect match to take on this new mission.

Jim was the Senior Cargo Specialist, in charge of lifts and drops for every ship using the Red Sands Space Port. He coordinated the usage of the three Space Elevators which, while tethered to the ground, were moored to their destinations at the cargo stations which remained in geosynchronous orbits. The elevators were held in place by using dense poly-carbon fibrous cable, both for ground retention and for the cable along which the elevators made their way for the entire two-hundred and twenty-five miles to the orbiting Space Station.

These magnificent inventions were first conceived back in the 1960's, but it took until 2050 for advances in technology to catch up with the capability of lifting cargo and people into space via an elevator. The cost savings in lifting cargo by elevators as opposed to using cold fusion drives, made the Red Sands Colony very wealthy.

Red Sands Space Port also served those, relatively small Space Shuttles capable of landing on the Red Planet. These were predominantly Space Defense Force Vessels, tourists, and immigrants. Cold fusion, which powers the Plasma drives, made for non-polluting landings and launches.

When Jim arrived, Reg invited him in and directed him to a seat. "Jim, I just got off the horn with Winters at the Trump Space Port in California. The comet mission is on, so let's kick the resupply of those freighters into high gear. They get top priority for anything they need. They're scheduled to leave orbit in, let's see, twenty-three hours and twenty-seven minutes."

Jim said, "Sure, Reg, we can make that happen, well, barring breakdowns and such. We've got all of their resupply on hand, so, yeah, we're good."

"Thanks, Jim, I appreciate how well you do what you do. Okay, you don't need me looking over your shoulder, so please, just git 'er done."

Jim Bream had worked for Reg Lee for nearly ten years, and though he was six years older than his boss, both men had a deep respect for each other. Hell, if Reg wants it done in twenty-three plus hours, then it will be done in twenty hours.

Jim had joined the Red Sands Colony in 2101, and once he became acclimated to Mars, the mere idea of ever returning to Earth caused a general unease. He told everyone that on Earth, he was running through chest-high water. His diaphragm heaved under the added stress of gravity until his lungs strengthened to breathe a bit more comfortably. His lungs convulsed as they spasmed for air, like a drowning Sunfish stranded on the dock. The damp and mildewy flavors of Earth brought discomfort to his nostrils and assaulted his taste buds, leaving a nearly uncontrollable urge to spit while wearing nose plugs.

Being a Martian, he thought the Earth was just too green, with way too many people. His place of origin was South Charleston, West

Virginia and he held a Master's Degree from West Virginia University. Reg often thought it funny that, while Jim had no desire to return to Earth, he tried to never miss a WVU Sporting Event and when his Mountaineers won Jim would strut around saying, "How 'bout them Eers."

MARCH 8, 2116, AD
GEO-SYNC ORBIT RED SANDS,
MARS COLONY

The senior Captain of the three freighters, currently in a geo-sync orbit over the Red Sands Space Port was Captain Scott King, though he allowed his few close friends to call him Sky King. He had come into space nearly forty years ago. He worked his way from Bridge Ensign to Captain in the Space Defense Force, and after thirty-five years, he retired.

During his tenure as Captain of the SDF Cruiser Wake Island, Captain King had gone toe to toe with the SRI-F Cruiser Lenin. The USUG-C and the SRI-F had managed to avoid war for forty years when the SRI-F decided to test the USUG-C resolve over discoveries on Mars. The SRI-F had demanded full access to the discovery of a Subterranean Martian city, dating back over ten million years.

The USUG-C denied the initial demand, citing potential corruption of the site. Full access would be granted once the city was mapped and cleaned.

Three weeks later, the RSN Cruiser Lenin appeared over the site and threatened to destroy it, should their demands for access be further denied.

Captain King placed his ship, the SDF Cruiser Wake Island between the Lenin and the Martian city. King ordered the Russians to withdraw.

Systemwide pressures grew dramatically as the Russians initially refused to budge and threatened to destroy the Wake Island if she continued to remain in the line of fire.

The talk of war was the only topic of conversation throughout the system. Both the USUG-C and the SRI-F ramped up military preparedness to Def-Con four. In orbit around Earth, ships of both Superpowers faced off and prepared for combat. On Earth, fleets began to sortie into open water. Armies and Reserves were called to duty. Global War seemed imminent, and global war was unthinkable.

As tensions rose, Captain King ordered that all weapons systems were to be kept fully powered up and prepared for battle.

Back on Earth, the United States President, Eileen N. Greene made it clear that the USUG-C would not allow the site to be destroyed, nor would SRI-F personnel be allowed on the site at the present time.

On day three of the Mexican stand-off, the Captain of the Lenin said, "Captain King, this is your last warning. Withdraw, or we will change you from the living to the dead."

Without missing a beat, Captain King responded with, "Boris, you couldn't change a dollar. Now, I will give you a fair warning; the instant our sensors detect you powering up any of your weapons systems, we will open fire."

On day four, the RSN Lenin withdrew.

The phrase, "You couldn't change a dollar," went viral and quickly became a part of American slang.

The US President told the Media in a Press Conference that the actions of Captain King were proper and thoroughly sanctioned by the

USUG-C. Greene told the reporters that she spoke with Captain King and congratulated him for his quick response to the Russian threat. His actions were in keeping with the most honored traditions of the Naval Service.

She ended the Press Conference with, "No Captain who, in service to his country, sails his vessel into harm's way is ever wrong."

Five years later, upon King's retirement, the ink wasn't dry on his papers when he was hired as Captain of the Mining Freighter, Astrid. Asteroid Mining Gmbh, a German company who had the foresight to begin mining the Asteroid Belt early on, was quick to grab Captain Sky King.

-

Captain King left his ready room and made his way to the Navigation Bridge.

As he entered, Lt JG Proud shouted, "Captain on Deck!"

"Afternoon, Pete," said the Captain, to the Watch Officer. "Please bring up the navigation charts showing our position, relative to Sol."

"Of course, sir, said Lt JG Peter Proud, Officer of the Day. Pete pulled up the hologram showing the location of the Red Planet in relation to the sun. "As you can see, Captain, we are near aphelion at a relative distance of around 1.45 AUs, roughly one-hundred and thirty million miles."

"Good, now bring up the current position of Holley Thorne, from our present location," ordered the Captain.

"Yes, sir, Holley Thorne is currently 2.09 AUs from Mars; our intercept time is one-hundred and eighty days, if we leave as scheduled on 9 March 2116. We will intersect with Holley Thorne on Sunday, 5 September 2116."

"Very well, send a message to Phobos and Deimos of the departure time, along with all pertinent data. Set your course, Pete, we depart in twenty-two hours," said Captain King.

"Aye, Captain," replied Lt. JG Peter Proud.

Back in the Captain's Ready Room, Sky King said, "Computer, direct Commander Ward to come to my Ready Room."

In less than two seconds the computer replied, "Message received. Commander Ward will arrive at your location in six minutes. He is currently located in loading dock three on J Deck."

"Fine, now contact Phobos and Deimos. Invite Captain's Putin and Chen to dinner this evening at 1900 hours."

"Yes, Captain, I'll let you know their response when they come in."

Unconsciously, King said, "Thank you," to his computer, who replied in a most pleasant female voice, "You are most welcome, Captain King."

Answering a damned computer, thought King, *why do I do that*?

"Wake up, JJ," said Sky to his AI, named in honor of Captain John Paul Jones.

Yes, Captain, how may I help?

"Send an email to my daughter, Hermione; say, I love you, Hermie. As you may now know I have been tasked with pushing the comet Holly Thorne away from the Earth and Moon. I have two other fine ships and crews to sort things out. I guess you know that this will put off our cruise vacation to Hawaii. I am sorry for that, but Holly Thorne just won't wait. I'm thinking of retiring after this mission, so go ahead and start planning on something really big.

"I hope you know that I am truly disappointed at missing our time together, but this is the mission I have spent my entire life preparing for, and it does seem like a fitting end to a truly satisfying career. Love ya, Sweetie. I'll see you in 2118. Love, Dad."

JJ said, *Got it, Captain. Will there be anything else?*

"Yes," said King, "check with the ship's computer and if Captain's Putin and Chen are coming for dinner this evening, contact the cook and lay on each man's favorite meal."

Yes, sir, I'm on it.

Commander Alan Ward arrived six minutes later. "Come on in, Al, and have a seat."

"Yes, sir, thank you, Captain, how may I be of assistance?"

King smiled and said, "Commander, we are going to war with Comet Holley Thorne. We clear the Space Dock in twenty-two hours. The particulars have been sent to your AI for perusal after the last of the provisions are secured. Speaking of which, how is our new Payload Master, Chief Jay Donovon shaping up."

Al smiled and said, "Sir, I am happy to report that he is exceeding my expectations. He doesn't need me looking over his shoulder, I'll still check in with him every few hours, or so anyway. He seems to be a real hard charger, why, is there something about him that I should know?"

"Actually, there is, Chief Donovon has turned down a commission three times. I'm not saying this as a possible conflict or concern, but I must say that I think there has to be a story there, somewhere."

"Oh, yes sir," smiled the XO, "when he received his welcome aboard interview, I asked him that exact question. His response was admirable. He said that he loved being the Payload Master and that he had no desire to take a job that put him behind a desk."

"How long has Donovon been a Payload Master, Al?" asked the Captain.

The XO said that his personnel file indicated that Chief Donovon had been an exemplary Payload Master for ten years. I think we struck gold with this one, Cap'n."

"Good, good, now, do you have any concerns about making our launch window?"

"No, sir, barring a breakdown, or mishap with the elevators, I see no problem."

The Captain looked at his XO and said, "Al, I know I run this ship like a US Space Defense Force Vessel, and now we'll be putting that training and discipline to effective use if we are going to bring this mission to a successful completion," said the Captain.

"Yes sir, personally, I have found your command presence to be refreshing. I have served on two other freighters, and from that experience, I have no question why the company put you in charge of this mission. Sir, your crew, is properly trained and ready to take on possibly the most important mission in the history of mankind."

"Yes, Al, that may be true, but I don't think we should pop the champagne corks just yet. Let's wait until we have a successful completion of mission to report."

"Yes, sir," said Al, "but you must admit that it is exciting to be a part of this endeavor."

Captain Sky King smiled and added, "Yes, Al, I do have to admit that I am both immensely excited and that I am scared to death, well, hopefully not to death.

"Holley Thorne is the largest comet that has ever been recorded, and that means that there will be plenty of rocks that will be thrown at us as she rotates on her axis. Every surface facing the sun will cast off pieces of itself as the Solar-side melts. Unfortunately, for us, we will have no real idea of her rotation speed or axis until we get up-close and personal. Keep everyone sharp, XO, this is one mission we cannot afford to screw up."

"Yes sir, I understand," replied the XO of The Mining Ship Astrid.

"All right, Al, let's get to work. Let me know when Captains Putin and Chen report readiness status."

"Roger, I'm on it, sir" and realizing he had been dismissed, the XO rose to return to his duties.

Holley Thorne continued her dive toward the star named Sol. She was monstrous, unrelenting, and dangerous. She would bypass all the planets of Sol by a wide margin, except for one Blue Marble in the system's Goldilocks Zone.

180 Days to Ship's Rendezvous with Holly Thorne

MARCH 9, 2116, AD
GEO-SYNC ORBIT, RED SANDS,
MARS COLONY

Seated in the Captain's Bridge Chair, the XO reported that both Phobos and Deimos were standing by for the launch command.

"Sir, all systems show nominal, we are ready to break station coupling and launch on your command."

"Thank you, XO, break coupling and take us out. We've got a comet to push around."

"Aye, aye, sir, Commo, inform Phobos and Deimos to follow us out. Helm, all ahead one Mars Standard."

"Aye, sir," parroted the Helmsman, "all ahead one Mars Standard."

Propulsion at one Mars Standard would maintain an artificial gravity equal to that of Mars. In six hours, the flotilla would begin increasing speed to 4.5 Mars Standards. The artificial gravity of one Mars Standard (MS) would be maintained by the ship's rotation. Twenty-five MS equated to 0.012 AU or forty-six thousand five-hundred miles per hour. It would take ten hours and twelve minutes to reach a speed of 0.012 AU.

MARCH 9, 2116, AD
HEINLEIN SPACE PORT
RED SANDS, MARS COLONY

Via video live-feed, Reg and his Space Port Payload Master watched the departure of the three-ship flotilla as they pulled away from the Space Station loading docks and began their journey to rendezvous with the comet Holly Thorne.

"Well, Jim," said Reg, "you did a terrific job in provisioning those three giants so quickly."

"Thanks, Reg, I appreciate that, but my people are well trained, and they did the job. I just stood around and bitched about getting the job done on time."

"Yeah, yeah," smiled Reg, "Whatever. Now, we wait and hope they can move that big bitch far enough outside of the moon's gravity to keep her from colliding with either the Moon or the Earth. Personally, I'm glad that we won't be passing through Holly's tail. I can't put my finger on it, but there's just something sinister about her."

Jim looked from the video and stared directly at Reg, saying, "I'm glad you mentioned that because I have that same nagging concern that something evil this way comes; glad I'm not the only one."

"Oh well, there's nothing more we can do for them, and we have a lot of ore to dispatch for processing," smiled Reg.

"Roger that, my friend and I'd better get to it or my boss will be on my ass."

Both men laughed as Reg said, "Damn straight, your boss is a slave driver."

CHAPTER THREE

727 Days until Holly Thorne passes Earth

Nighty Night!

9 MARCH 2116
WHITE HOUSE
MOSCOW, SRI-F HQ

The private Conference Room of the Chairman, Admiral of the Fleet, Victor Sokolov sat with the Indian, Admiral of the Fleet, Akash Paliath Achan, and the Chinese, Admiral First Class Liu Bang.

Each man had an AI that maintained the instant translation of his counterparts. The AI also managed to remove the distracting voices of the foreign languages. The Admirals only heard their own language.

"My friends," said Sokolov, we must ensure that this monster which threatens the Earth is destroyed, should the SDF be unable to push the comet out of Luna's path. Beyond that, however, I believe that we might have an opportunity here, to inflict some damage to our most arrogant adversaries, caused by the Comet Holley Thorne, of course." This caused all three men to laugh at the thought of humbling the all mighty Americans and their lackeys, the British and the Germans.

"I propose that we dispatch a fleet of seven ships to intersect the Comet. Once we are on-site, we shall evaluate the need for firing nuclear missiles into the heart of Holly Thorne, and perhaps a couple of missiles just a bit too close to the accursed USSDF Fleet.

"That far out in space, their ships will have no possible way to contact their Fleet Headquarters to tell them of the terrible accident, because we will block all communications until they are all dead, and these fools will lose 70% of their entire fleet in a matter of one millisecond. In space, a near miss is a thousand miles, enough to irradiate their entire fleet."

These were men of power and influence. They were not accustomed to others questioning their decisions, and as each man harbored an unbridled hatred of the USSDF, consensus came easily.

Over lunch and small talk, the decision was made to dispatch the entire SRI-F Fleet in two increments of three and four vessels. The lead element would depart on 19 March 2116, with the remaining ships following one week later. They would sail under the command of Captain Nicolay Volodin. Each member nation would provide their ships.

170 Days to Ship's Rendezvous with Holly Thorne

19 MARCH 2116
CAPTAIN'S READY ROOM
ASTEROID MINING VESSEL ASTRID

Captain King looked over his Officers, Senior Chiefs, and the holograms of Captain's Putin and Chen, before saying, "I appreciate the outstanding job you have each done in preparing us for the mission ahead. Job one complete, but now it's time to climb into those charming sleep chambers we all have grown to love so well," said a somewhat sarcastic Captain Sky King.

"All crew members will enter the chambers, less the skeleton Bridge, and Engineering Staff, at 2200 hours this cycle. We will be awakened at 0700 hours on 28 August, seven days before the rendezvous with Holly Thorne. Are there any questions?"

There were no questions, as every spacer aboard these three ships knew his job. King said, "All right then, we'll meet here in 163 days at 1000 hours. Good night, good luck, and let's do this. Dismissed."

At 2200 hours on 19 March 2116, the ships fell silent, but for the caretaker crews assigned to maintain a vigil in case something went wrong.

717 Days to Earth

28 MARCH 2116
WHITE HOUSE OVAL OFFICE
WASHINGTON, DC

Tessa Van Horn, President Eileen Greene's Secretary, buzzed into the Oval Office.

"Yes?" answered the President.

"Madame President, the Chief of Staff, and Mr. Gordon Winters, the NASA Director, just called and asked if you might have five minutes available for an update on Operation HT."

"When can he be here?" asked Eileen.

"Ma'am, they're in the Chief's Office, now."

"Oh, I see, did he say it was urgent?"

"No, ma'am, Mr. Gordon just finished another meeting with the Chief of Staff, and they both thought you'd like the latest on the Holly Thorne mission."

"All right, Tess, tell them to come on down, then move everything on the calendar forward by twenty minutes."

"Yes, ma'am," said Tessa.

Five minutes later both the COS, retired Lt. General Harry Wolfe, and the NASA Director, Gordon Winters were ushered into the Oval Office.

President Greene said, "Well, Harry, I hope you and Gordon have good news, because today, I can surely use some."

Both men smiled and took the proffered seats before the President's desk. General Wolfe said, "Actually ma'am, we have both good and possibly not so good news."

"Oh, crap, come on, Harry, out with it, and don't ask which I want first, good or bad, just spit it out. I still have a couple of nerves which are not completely frazzled this afternoon."

The two men chuckled politely at the President's humor before Harry said, "Okay, bad news first; at 1300 local time, the SRI-F (Sino-Russian-Indian Federation) launched three vessels on an apparent intercept of Holly Thorne from their orbiting Base Station. Wait, it gets worse. SRI-F says they plan to launch four more vessels for rendezvous with Holly Thorne." The COS paused for effect, and President Greene asked, "Does it get worse?"

"Yes, ma'am, it does. All vessels are armed with rail guns and nuclear missiles."

"Oh, hell. Harry, make an appointment with the SRI-F COS and see if you can learn anything about their intentions. If you get no satisfaction, then make an appointment with the SRI-F President so I can speak with him personally."

"Yes, ma'am," said, the COS, "I'll get on it right after this meeting."

"How long until they reach our mining ships?" asked Eileen.

"Their estimated time to HT intercept is November 15th of this year. Our flotilla will have only been pushing on Holly Thorne for about nine weeks. It will take a total of no less than ten months to push Holly safely outside the Lunar orbit."

"Oh, joy," quipped the President, "aren't you just a ray of sunshine on this dreary day? Okay, is there anything else you have to report, General Buzz Kill?"

"No, nothing terrible, at least for the moment.

Gordon, your turn up to bat," smiled the COS.

"Yes, sir, Madame President, I am happy to report that the launch of the three mining ships assigned to move Holly Thorne entered their Sleep Chambers, on schedule, and will be awakened on 28 August. This gives them a seven-day window to make final preparations to engage Holly. Plus, it allows sufficient time to reverse course and take station along the port side of the comet.

"We have successfully inserted a virus that we have named Thirty-Eight Protocol, into the computer drives. Once activated, Thirty-Eight Protocol will take complete control of the ship's drive. The vessels will then be diverted to thirty-eight degrees from the ecliptic at maximum warp and placed on a course which will, in two years take the ships into the sun. Captain King will read his special orders concerning Holly Thorne when he is awakened from his Sleep Chamber on 28 August."

"Tell me, Harry, will he do it?" asked President Greene.

"Ma'am, Sky King is old-time Space Navy. I have no doubt, whatsoever, that he will do his duty should the need arise. Now, having said that, we can also initiate the virus from Earth. Personally, my money is on Captain Sky King to do what needs to be done," replied the COS.

"Thank you, gentlemen, for your appraisals and candor. It has only just occurred to me, but couldn't China, et al., assist our ships in pushing Holly around?"

Gordon answered, saying, "Unfortunately, Madame President, their Space Forces, like ours, do not have the lasers necessary for the job. They also do not have the standoff armor of the Asteroid Mining Vessels."

"Well, darn, it would have made things so much easier if they could have joined the effort as part of a coalition," said Eileen. "Now, I suppose we'll be forced to allow our SDF to join the parade, to protect the flotilla and prevent those three hammers from trying to put nuclear nails into Holly Thorne."

The COS, General Wolfe said, "Ma'am, I have directed the seven SDF vessels now in orbit around Mars to be prepared to join Captain King. They are standing by for launch orders."

"Well done, Harry. Go ahead and send 'em out. Gentlemen, is there anything else?"

"Just one thing Madame President," said Harry, "are you going to meet with the Space Force Congressional Committee, concerning these developments?"

"Yes, I don't have any other choice, do I? I'll have Tess call Congressman Melvin Norton. I'll give him the rundown, oh, and both you and NASA need to be on hand, too. God, but I hate that man."

The two men, realizing that they were being dismissed rose to leave. As NASA left the office, the COS shut the door and said, "Eileen, I have some concern that both of the remaining Captains of our flotilla are natives of the SRI-F. I'm not saying this means anything, but we must not lose sight of any rogue possibilities. I also want to Federalize all crew members of the mining ships and bring them into the SDF. I'd like to allow Captain King to decide whether he should keep the Russian and Chinese Captains on as Contract employees."

"Thank you, Harry; take what precautions you feel are necessary to ensure their loyalty to the mission. Tell me, Harry, why do you always have to stir up so much crap?"

As he reached for the doorknob, a grinning COS said, "Like the old saying goes, I know, ma'am, it's a dirty job, but somebody has to do it."

Eileen just smiled and shook her head as Harry exited the Oval Office.

2116
EARTH

Life continued unabated and generally unconcerned over the potential catastrophe hurtling toward the Earth. Most people saw the comet as too far away to pay much attention to its approach. News networks focused on the Politicians running for office during mid-term Legislative Elections, and how the balance of power in the US could change.

China, Russia, and India made up the Federation (SRI-F) that represented the primary rivals of the US, United Kingdom, and Germany Coalition (USUG-C). Each of these two Super Powers had a myriad of

Vassal States that seemed to scurry about the skirts of these two rival powers.

The SRI-F had initially, tentatively agreed not to attack Holly Thorne, but then quickly sent ships carrying nuclear weapons, ostensibly to observe the progress of the USUG-C efforts to push the comet away from any possible collision course with Earth or Luna.

The internet, however, was a different matter as the Conspiracy Theorists were abuzz with several tales of woe. Some claimed unnamed authorities had learned that the comet was being guided by Aliens to destroy life on Earth unless all governments surrendered. Earth would become a non-space faring, agrarian society governed by an alien coalition determined to end the threat of Human expansion into the galaxy.

Others proclaimed that God was behind Holly Thorne's approach. According to them, Mankind had until March 4th, 2118 to become worthy to receive God's Grace. Failing to receive His Grace, the Rapture would occur on March 5th of 2118. God would then destroy the Earth on the following day.

Others claimed Satan had gained control and would begin the Tribulations. One conspiracy theorist actually hit the nail directly on the head when he reported the Spanish Flu Pandemic of 1918 was the result of the Earth passing through the tail of a comet.

But, on the whole, life went on just as it always had.

Mount Weather and Cheyenne Mountain, however, quietly continued their preparations for Holly's arrival.

29 MARCH 2116
CHURCH OF THE LIGHT
PHILADELPHIA, PA

The lights shining down on the Altar seemed just a bit dimmer than in previous services. The Choir sang soft, melodious hymns of bygone days. The air began to stir as the thousands in attendance began to sense something was about to happen; something wild, yet wonderful.

Pastor Elijah Wright sat silent and still in his chair after being announced for what seemed an eternal minute, raising the sense of drama. Finally, he arose and walked to center stage. He stood before his congregation of more than six-thousand. His message began slowly, almost in a whisper, yet building with each new phrase until he was shouting a venom-filled sermon. A sermon calling for everyone who was not currently seated in his church to be sent directly to the fiery lakes of Hell.

He ranted about God's will and how man had turned against Him, rejecting His Grace and His love of man."

Throwing his right arm toward the Heavens, his hand holding an old and worn Bible, Wright's voice emoted confidence in his words, "Jehovah is a jealous God, and He has been unhappy for some time at mankind's rejection. Now, He throws a cold, frozen and dirty snowball at us. A snowball that will bring fire and brimstone in its wake. My friends, we cannot avoid God's wrath."

His voice once again dropped to a conversational, yet deadly serious tone, saying, "We must accept the End Times message of Holly Thorne. My children, fellow believers, we must rally with protests in the streets, demanding that we must not further anger the Almighty by attempting to interfere with His comet which comes our way. If it is within our power, we demand that Holly Thorne is left alone to complete her mission."

Wright's voice revealed a growing passion as he said, "Oh, yes! I feel the presence of our Great God Jehovah. He is here among us on this day, at this very moment. He speaks to me. He says…"

At this point of Wright's sermon, his body suddenly jerks frantically, and he falls to his knees. He screams, "Hallelujah, yes my Father I hear you!"

Several members of the assemblage and the Choir began to move to the Reverend, thinking he was in distress.

"Stand back," he shouts, "for the Lord God is speaking to me! Yes, Father, I understand, and I will obey."

The Altar lights begin to brighten, taking on a vague, golden hue. Wright then opened his eyes and slowly raised his head to the congregation. His now bright eyes sought the heavens, and his face was forever changed. He slowly raised himself to his feet, still seeking the face of God. Once he was fully standing, he looked at those gathered in His name, as though for the first time, and speaking in a calm, even voice, said, "My children, Reverend Wright has been taken by a Heavenly Chariot to receive his reward. He is now, as we speak meeting my Father. I am your Beloved Lord and Savior, Yeshua. This was my name during my time on Earth, as I walked among men. You know me through the translation of Yeshua, from Aramaic to Jesus Christ, in English."

Several women fell to their knees and shouted *Hallelujah, praise God.*

Ushers stood on each side of the Chapel doors, and when one man rose to leave, he was stopped when Wright raised his hand, and the Chapel doors slammed shut. The Ushers jumped from the startling thunderclap of sound as the two doors slammed shut. They fell to their knees in supplication.

"Be seated, my son," said Wright, in a warm and forgiving lilt, "for I have come to deliver great and joyous news to the righteous among you. I say unto you that you must act in accordance with my Father's divine and moral law. You must remain free from guilt or sin. I bring you the morally right and justifiable path you must undertake to prepare for the Jubilee of my return to Earth. I have been sent by my Father, your God, Jehovah, not as a Prince of Peace, but as a Warrior Prince.

"You are called upon to pave the way to Paradise; as it is written in 1st Thessalonians 4:17. Then we, which are alive and remain shall be caught up together with them in the clouds, to meet the Lord in the air: and so shall we ever be with the Lord, FOR THE RAPTURE OF THE LORD IS NIGH! I HAVE RETURNED! AND YE SHALL REJOICE, FOR YE ARE IN THE ONE TRUE CHURCH OF THE LIGHT! Brothers and Sisters in the Choir, please sing We Shall Arise."

At this point the Choir and church members erupted into song, and delight, as their Savior walked among them, touching them, healing their hearts and minds.

The Choir sang;

> *We shall arise to meet in the sky*
> *When Gabriel blows his trumpet loud,*
> *No more the grave will us enshroud*
> *There will be no sorrow,*
> *there on that glad morrow*
> *Yes, when the trumpet shall sound, we shall arise…*

As the music ended Wright said, "Brother Emmanuel, recite this Psalm." Wright again raised his arm, palm outward, directed to the

Deacon named Emmanuel. The Deacon reeled back as though struck by the hand of Jesus. Upon recovery, and without being told which Psalm to recite he began, "Yea, though I walk…"

The Congregation was now in a fever-pitched state of rapturous joy. Several women swooned or fainted. Some said it was mostly his glowing eyes that seemed to have changed, while other swore it was his face which took on a glow of righteousness. His stride was straight and strong, his voice clear and pure. This Assemblage would never doubt, or deny, their Messiah. What he demanded, they would provide.

Later, over brandy and cigars, Wright and his Inner Circle laughed as he said, "These people are morons. All it took was a little lighting, slamming doors, contacts, a little makeup, and some good acting on our part to make them believe I am Jesus. Gentlemen, I give you the first recruits of a new army which will sweep the world…LaVonne, go ahead and release the video."

CHAPTER FOUR

7 Days to Ship's Rendezvous with Holly Thorne

28 AUGUST 2116, 0700
ABOARD THE ASTRID

The crews were awakened, and the men and women of the flotilla began stretching to relieve stiffened muscles and joints. A common discussion among the crews when they were released from their Sleep Chambers was, "Did you dream?" Some said yes, while most had no memory of any dreams. Quickly, the ship's personnel scheduled for the first watch were heading to their stations.

Even a week away, Holly Thorne was clearly visible, and as the two forces drew closer, the immensity of the job of pushing this behemoth would be more difficult than initially thought. Holly Thorne's axis rotation was not what was expected. Her rotation was forty-five degrees from the ecliptic, and she wobbled erratically.

This combination of forces caused Holly to throw off debris in every conceivable direction. The hope had been for a nice level rotation which would throw the predominance of Holly Thorne's excretions to starboard, in relation to the orbit around Sol. Had this been the case, the three ships planned to place themselves alongside the comet on the Port side, keeping them in relative safety.

Captain King held a holographic meeting with Putin and Chen. "Gentlemen, this is going to be a bit more of an opportunity to excel than we had hoped. I know that I am glad that we are so well armored because it will be impossible for us to avoid all of Holly's knuckleballs."

Captains Putin and Chen now had grave misgivings about the possibility of success. Captain King agreed but reminded them that grave misgivings meant nothing, as the mission must be successfully completed.

"Gentlemen, we will stand off from this monster at a distance of fifty-thousand miles. This should give us an hour to make adjustments for any large rocks she throws at us."

The discussion lasted another ten minutes but became a bull shit session after five. King let them chat on for another five minutes before ending the mission brief.

"Well, Al, the die is cast, so let's get to work. Get us positioned at fifty-thousand miles from Miss Holly Thorne on the port side. I want this job underway as soon as we come on-station, Roger?"

"Yes, sir," said the XO, "Roger that."

The three ships were beehives of activity over the next seven days, checking and rechecking every piece of equipment on board. Off-duty time was spent around several video rooms where the approach of Holly Thorne was constantly streamed. Holly was growing on the video screens at an impressive rate.

The comet's Tail stretched well beyond the orbit of Saturn. On 4 September 2116, the three vessels attained portside station with Holly Thorne. Four days before meeting Holly Thorne, the three ships of Earth's Flotilla put on the brakes and began to reverse course, matching the comet.

0 Days to Ship's Rendezvous with Holly Thorne

4 SEPTEMBER 2116, 0700
50,000 MILES OFF THE PORT SIDE OF THE COMET
ABOARD THE ASTRID

Klaxons sounded throughout the ship, "Captain to the Bridge!" came the call from Astrid's Communication Station. Captain King leaped to his feet and opened his Ready Room door and onto the Bridge.

"Captain on the Bridge!" shouted the XO.

Taking the Bridge Captain's chair, King said, "Status, XO."

"Captain, we are on station and ready to commence operations. However, seven ships are approaching, nearly two days behind us. They have identified themselves as USSDF vessels, and our Foof (Friend or Foe) Transponder concurs, sir."

"I see, now I wonder why we have received such an impressive escort. XO, this can only mean that Sino-Russia-India Federation (SRI-F) armed vessels are also on the way."

"Yes, sir, that is exactly what I believe to be true. Your orders, Captain?"

King thought for a moment before saying, "Contact the SDF vessels and tell them to lay off at a distance of seventy-thousand miles from the comet. Contact Putin and Chen to make them aware of the SDF presence."

"Shall I also mention the possibility of SRI-F forces entering the arena?" asked the XO.

"No, not until we know for sure. In the interim, have your AI dig up the deep personnel dossiers on Putin and Chen. If there is any problem gaining access, my AI will run interference for you, Roger, JJ?"

Of course, sir, Roger that.

"Now, for the historical record," King said, "Commander Ward, commence operation Holly Thorne."

"Aye Captain, Chief of the Boat Harkins, commence firing."

"Aye, aye Commander, commencing operation Holly Thorne, light her up, boys."

And with that command, all three ships trained their lasers on the comet and began heating the port side of Holly Thorne, pushing her away from Earth.

King chuckled and said, "Well, *light her up, boys* may not be up there with *one giant leap for mankind,* but I like it. Pass my appreciation on to Chief of the Boat Harkins, XO. All right, resume normal operations and stand down from Lifeboat drill. I'll tell you, XO, I have a feeling that when those Klaxons ring in the future it will be for Battle Stations."

"Yes, sir, that could be. I certainly hope not, but it could be," replied the XO.

"Communications, contact Earth at JPL and advise them we have commenced Operation Holly Thorne."

"Roger, sir, sending message to JPL, now."

"Anything else, sir?"

"No XO, you have the Bridge." I'm going to my Ready Room for some quiet study."

"Aye Captain, I have the Bridge," parroted the XO.

Once the commencement of operations phase was recorded for posterity, the Astrid shut down her lasers and fell into a three-ship rotation. This rotation would result in two ships firing into the comet, allowing a cool-down period for the off-duty lasers.

"Well, JJ, it's time," said Sky to his AI.

Yes, Captain King, it is finally time.

"Tell me, JJ, did you also sleep during transit?"

Oh, no sir. I remained on duty monitoring both your health as well as the ships for the entire transit.

When the Captain returned to his Ready Room, JJ said, *Captain King, I have a side channel message from Admiral Perry. It was sent just after you went into your Sleep Chamber and locked from my awareness protocol until just one moment ago. Shall I read it now?*

"Yes, JJ, go ahead."

TOP SECRET, CRYPTO

Captain Scott King- NO DESSEMINATION / EYES ONLY

Message reads, from, U.S.S.D.F., Red Sands, Mars

Vice Admiral Adolphus Perry,

Commanding

Subject: Mission safeguards.

Congratulations Captain King on the successful initiation of Operation HT.

By order of the President of the United States, President Eileen N. Greene, I have been ordered to give you an emergency, system-wide, computer protocol which will give you total, and unalterable helm control of all three vessels should the need arise. This computer upgrade was downloaded while your crews were in the Sleep Chambers.

As we have no idea of any potential threat HT may pose in this regard, this safety protocol was uploaded so that, should you be confronted by a situation in which your flotilla becomes a danger to Earth, you must initiate helm control. Should you be incapacitated, this override will be directed from HQ SDF.

This control will place your command at maximum thrust on a course of thirty-eight degrees from the ecliptic. This action will take you on an unalterable course out of the Solar System to a point directly above the Sun from the ecliptic. Your ships will then alter course and plunge directly into Sol. This course will take two years, at which time your command will be unmanned derelicts.

Please reference the 1918 Spanish Flu pandemic which coincided with the Earth's passage through the tail of another comet.

Should your ships fall prey to a similar pandemic, and subsequent loss of life, I urge you to save the lives of billions of human beings on Earth by issuing the following command through your AI:

I I f I l w y (69), King, Scott A, confirmed.

Respond via your AI confirmation of your receipt of this message.

Sky, I pray this order will never be needed, but you have this option should it become necessary.

God Speed, my friend,

Dolph

Adolphus Perry

Vice Admiral,

USUGC Space Defense Force, Commanding

"JJ, did you record the code to memory?"

Yes, Sky, I have it. How would you like me to execute this protocol should the situation arise?

"JJ, you are directed to run Thirty-Eight Protocol on my command prompt of, 'JJ, execute Thirty-Eight Protocol'. If the ship's crew becomes incapacitated from an unknown virus and if I am also incapacitated due to an illness, or if I am within moments of my death and not able to give the command, I order you to run Thirty-Eight Protocol. Remember, JJ, the command will be Thirty-Eight Protocol, not thirty-eighth or protocols. Does that make sense to you? It's important that the command is 'Thirty-Eight Protocol.'"

Yes, I understand, and I will, of course, comply with your instruction to initiate Thirty-Eight Protocol.

"Good man, JJ. Contact Vice Admiral Perry with an encrypted message, eyes only, CDR. USSDF. 'I have received info on Thirty-Eight Protocol. I understand and accept responsibility for execution.'

"Dolph, I sure hope it doesn't come to that, but I don't want my Hermie to die because I failed in my duty to protect our people. Please check on her for me. Thanks, Sky."

Yes, sir, message sent, but I must remind you that I am an AI, not a man.

"Shut up JJ, and don't call me Sky."

Shutting up, sir.

4 SEPTEMBER 2116, AD
ON STATION
50,000 MILES PORT SIDE OF HOLLY THORNE

Captain King, I have just received a communication from the AI of Vice Admiral Adolphus Perry Commander of the U. S. Space Force (USSDF). Shall I read it to you, now?

"What?" exclaimed King. "You must be having a malfunction. That is just not possible at this distance."

Sir, I just ran a diagnostic and found a new file on my memory card. Apparently, this file was downloaded during my last update, three days ago. Shall I read it to you, now?

Dumbfounded, King said, "Yeah, sure, go ahead JJ, please read it to me."

TOP SECRET CRYPTO

Captain Scott King - EYES ONLY

Commanding Asteroid Mining Vessel Astrid and Task Force Holly Thorne

From: Commander USSDF, Vice Admiral Adolphus R. Perry

*To: Captain *(P) Scott A. King*

1. *Subject: Recall to Active Service with USSDF*
    i.   *all U.S.U.G.C. crew members of Vessels Astrid, Phobos, and Deimos drafted into service with USSDF*
    ii. *Previous Presidential contractual agreements remain intact for all personnel.*
2. *Captains Putin, Chen, and citizens of nations other than the U.S., U.K., and Germany are offered civilian contracts to serve with the USSDF*

"WHAT? JJ are you jerking my chain?" asked an astounded Sky King.

"No, sir, shall I continue?

"Oh, yes, sorry for the interruption; go ahead."

"Yes, sir."

Scott, I know this is a shock, but tensions are building between SRI-F and the U.S., UK, and German Confederation (USUG-C).

Good news first: You are at this moment, upon receipt of this message promoted to the rank of Rear Admiral, to serve until the current crisis is resolved, plus six months.

Your XO is promoted to Captain, so it's your fleet, Admiral. Select additional promotion among your new command as you deem appropriate.

Okay, now the unpleasant news. SRI-F has sent two flotillas, one, consisting of three vessels which departed their Space Station the day after you went into the Sleep Chambers, and the second of four vessels departed one week later. Scott, these vessels are all heavily armed with rail-guns and nukes.

Our seven-vessel fleet is similarly armed and should arrive on 30 August. Captain Jessica Flynn, commanding Leyte Gulf, is in temporary command until your meeting with her and she hand delivers the assumption of command and the promotion orders to you, personally. She will have appropriate duty uniforms for all hands

Additionally, two USUG-C cargo vessels, departed for your location one week after the SRI-F ships left Earth. They, like the SDF warships, departed from Red Sands, Mars. These transports are carrying rail-guns and munitions for your mining vessels. With your armor, you should have the three most powerful ships in the system. As the SRI-F Fleet departed from Earth, you should have ample time to train-up your gunnery crews.

Your job is now expanded to push Holly Thorne's big ass out of the way, and to take command of the USSDF Fleet. Scott, you must defend that comet. We must not allow it to be blown into large pieces that could endanger Earth.

Captains Putin and Chen must be watched closely. Hell, I have no idea where their sympathies lie.

Should you need to replace them, SDF Marines will board their vessels and transfer them to SDF Brigs. If this is necessary, please consider transferring them to SRI-F authorities upon their arrival as a goodwill gesture.

Scott, I have sent this message via our AIs for two reasons: I do not want Putin or Chen to see it, and the second reason is that the SRI-F has not developed AI thought transmission over distances of one hundred yards. Commo between SRI-F Vessels and their Commands now takes approximately thirty-five minutes. This lag time gives us a slim communications advantage.

As our new beta version of AI thought-communication appears to be near instantaneous, you have received this message pretty darned quick, considering you are thirty-five light-minutes away.

Well, Admiral, there you have it, down and dirty. I just hope you have a habitable Earth to come home to.

Oh, yes, don't worry about Hermie, Louise is keeping in near constant contact with her. Relax about her, we've got this.

Good luck, my old friend,
Dolph

*(P = Promotable)

PS: I know how surprised you are to be getting this message from me; our techies have managed to pull this miracle off, and this is the beta version. Scott, there are only two AIs with the download anywhere. That's you and me, pal. Don't tell anyone! SRI-F has no idea we can communicate in this way. They are bound by any orders given before their departure. Let's keep it that way.

Our techies think we should shut down the communication except for designated contact times. JJ must find his internal dipswitch which will shut down our communications. Our designated contact times are 0600, 1200, and 1800, your time.

Admiral; that completes the message. Would you like for me to read it again?

"Uh, no, send a classified reply advising the Admiral of my receipt of his message. Also include the somewhat sarcastic reply of 'Gee thanks, Dolph', and sign it Sky."

"I found the switch; shall I turn it off for now?

"Yes, JJ, well done. Now, delete all portions of the message which gives any information on how it was transmitted to me. Then contact the XO's AI and have him report ASAP to my Ready Room."

"Done."

Al knocked on the Admiral's Ready Room door and was directed in.

"Yes, sir," said the XO, is there something you need?"

"Yes, Al, but you might go ahead and sit down first."

"Yes, sir, is it that bad?"

Admiral King said, "Well, that depends on your perspective, but overall, it ain't good. While we were in transit from Red Sands, my AI,

JJ received sealed orders concerning this mission. I am going to have JJ transmit a TOP SECRET CRYPTO EYES-ONLY MESSAGE to your AI. A more formal, edited version is with Captain Jessica Flynn, commanding the USSDF Cruiser Leyte Gulf. Ready?"

"Yes, sir, of course."

Al's face turned from shock and dismay to acceptance as his AI read the letter. A smile came to his face at the point of hearing about his promotion.

"Holy crap, Admiral, things must be getting really bad back home. Are we about to get into a real gut-busting shooting war?"

Sky looked distracted and said, "Al, I hope not, but I just don't know."

"Wait a minute. Admiral, how did you say you received this message?"

"Al, the message was transmitted on a classified ultra-high-frequency AI band. You will receive one later in the mission. The receipt time is roughly two times that of regular radar projected commo. I know it is an old cliché, but it's true that if I told you more than that, I would have to kill you. So, don't ask, or try to guess. Understood?

"Roger, sir, understood."

"All right, I want you to contact the SDF Commander, Captain Flynn. Send my compliments to her and arrange for me to visit her flagship.

I guess we'll also need to schedule a formal dinner the following day for all Ship's Captains, at, oh, let's see, yeah, make it for 1900 hours."

"Of course, sir, when and at what time for your meet with Captain Flynn?"

The new Admiral said, "I guess sooner is better than later, and let's make it over dinner.

Oh, yes, contact her XO and arrange for their Stores Officer to send over our new uniforms. You're in the Navy now, son."

"Yes, sir. I guess that begs the question of how our relationship, both militarily and personal is going to change."

"Yes, I suppose you're right. How does this sound? In private we'll continue as we have been. In front of others, look sharp."

"Thank you, sir, that sounds fine. Will you be moving your new flag to one of the SDF Vessels?"

"I'm not sure. The quarters on this barge are better than those SDF ships. Still, if Flynn bitches about it, I will have to, since she has seniority and an SDF Cruiser. We'll see. Now, I want you to recommend who you want as your new XO since you'll be taking over command of the Astrid."

"Yes, sir, I'll get the promotions and roster changes to you before 1700 hours."

"If 1700 interferes with dinner, 0800 hours is fine. Let's get Lieutenant JG Proud on that promotion list."

"Roger sir, he was already high on the list for L T."

"Alan," said Admiral King, "don't forget that deep data search on Putin and Chen. See what you can dig up to help figure where they will stand.

While Al was doing his research on Putin and Chen, Sky dove into the records of the SDF Captains. Following this, he did a classified search of the new class of Washington Class Cruisers and their armaments.

The primary offensive weapon systems were railguns and plasma torpedoes. Railgun munitions have no explosives. The weapon fired granite-like projectiles at horrendous speeds. Their impact alone caused massive damage to any ship hit by railgun munitions. The plasma torpedoes were another story entirely as there was no armor known to man that could prevent the destruction of any ship struck by this weapon.

Many a young cadet at the USSDF Academy on Luna asked why the SDF continued to use rail guns when the plasma torpedo was so much more destructive. After all, the railgun was not a guided munition. The Academy Teaching Staff always answered the same way.

"We have not yet reached the technology to allow rapid regeneration of the power required to fire large numbers of plasma torps. The destructive power of the railgun is, however, also devastating, and the ammunition for them can easily be produced by the ship's crew by mining, melting, and forming millions of railgun munitions from nearby asteroids very quickly.

"Yes, the railgun is more like a shotgun, since the rounds are not guided, and if detected, the targeted ship has a good chance of moving away from the trajectory of an oncoming rail gun round."

The same students would always then ask the same question, "Then why do we use them?"

Instructors would then smile and say, "Yes, a targeted ship may well be able to avoid one round, but not so much with one-hundred thousand rounds coming their way. Nearly two-hundred years ago, a Russian Dictator named Josef Stalin was reported to have said, quantity has a quality all its own. In this case, he was absolutely correct."

"Sir," an eager Cadet would always ask, "how fast does a rail gun round travel in space?"

"That information is classified, but it is around two hundred miles per second."

This response, of course, brought excited exchanges of USSDF power, until one student would inevitably ask, in an almost muted voice, "How fast are the SRI-F railgun rounds?"

"We believe them to be exactly the same."

That single comment always ended any questions about railgun use in space combat. A typical math equation was drilled into each Cadet's brain. It was simple but imperative; as space combat is anticipated to be at ranges beyond one-hundred thousand miles, how long will it take for the first railgun round to be on target? This simple formula was $((d/s)/60=tot.)$

Written out, it becomes:

((distance to target divided by the speed of munition assuming a speed of two hundred miles per second) divided by sixty seconds equaling the time in minutes and seconds to time-on-target). Ergo, a target sitting one-hundred thousand miles away would take eight point three minutes to impact, or time-on-target.

Each USSDF Cruiser carried a complement of one-hundred rail guns, mounted around the ship in shielded blisters, sixteen plasma torpedo launch tubes, twelve forward and four aft, for offensive weaponry.

The USSDF Cruiser was three-thousand two-hundred and seventy-six feet long, and one-thousand feet across her beam. Each Cruiser's crew consisted of fifteen-thousand spacers, including a battalion of five-hundred Space Marine's. The twelve R4W Cold-Fusion power plants were designed to keep the ship in-service without a refit for sixty years.

The Mining Vessels were of similar size but were crewed by only twelve-thousand spacers. These ships held huge cargo bays for storing ore and supplies, including nearly five-hundred spare 1,000 kWh lasers. Even in space, these behemoths maneuvered like wallowing pigs.

Forty minutes later, the XO reported that Alexi Putin was very much vocally disparaging of the Russian Empire. Chen, however, seemed very supportive of China and there was a one-year gap in Chen's history.

Captain Flynn dispatched the uniforms for Admiral King, and Captain Ward, to allow them to be in proper attire for the meetings and dinner.

The two visiting Captains were guided to King's Ready Room. When they saw Sky King and Alan Ward dressed in their new SDF uniforms, Putin asked in a heavy Russian accent, "Well, well, Admiral, are you going to a costume party. Are we invited?"

"Of course, you are." smiled the Admiral, "Gentlemen, please take a seat, we have much to discuss."

Captain Chen Feng (last name first in Chinese culture) was far more cautious as he scrutinized the SDF uniforms.

King spent several minutes explaining the new orders he had received via Captain Flynn, thus avoiding the AI communications breakthrough.

"…Well, gentlemen, there you have it. You may remain as the Captains of your vessels, but under a Civilian Contract offered by the SDF, or if you decline, you will remain in your current position of Captain until the arrival of the SRI-F. At that point, I am bound to allow you to resign your position as Captain. You will then be transferred to an SRI-F vessel when they arrive. You don't have to answer right now. Think it over and get back to me. The SRI-F Fleet won't arrive for another nine months, or so."

Chen agreed to consider the offer, but Alexi Putin said, "Admiral, I do not need to think about this for even one second. Of course, I accept your offer. I have no desire to ever again serve those Russian bastards or eat Borsht. I hate bitter foods, especially soup."

It was agreed that Captain Flynn would make the presentation to the crews, informing them of the draft, though it was possible that many might think they had been Shanghaied.

The mining shuttle craft departed Astrid and flew along and around the SDF Cruiser Leyte Gulf before docking so that Sky King could see firsthand the external changes to SDF vessels since his retirement.

5 SEPTEMBER 2116, AD
INSPECTING USSDF LEYTE GULF' EXTERIOR
70,000 MILES PORT SIDE OF HOLLY THORNE

Admiral King delayed his formal meeting with Captain Flynn, and the six other Captains until 5 September 2116, to give everyone the chance to get fully recovered from the Sleep Chambers and properly situated on-station.

"Computer," said the Admiral.

Yes, Admiral, ready.

"Please inform Captain's Putin and Chen that I wish an in-person meeting aboard Astrid in one hour."

Yes, Admiral, message sent.

"Thank you."

You are welcome, Admiral.

"Oh, crap," said King, "I said thank you to the damned computer again. I gotta stop that. It's making me crazy."

Captain Ward just smiled. JJ said, *Admiral, I'm a computer, and you speak to me."*

"Shut up, JJ."

Shutting up, Admiral.

"JJ giving you a tough time, Admiral?" asked Captain Ward.

The Admiral looked at Captain Al Ward and said, "Not really, it's just our love-hate relationship."

"Oh, yes, sir," replied Al, "I have the same thing with JD."

"JD, why JD?" asked Sky.

"Yeah, well, when my AI was implanted the programmer asked me for a name, and John D. MacDonald was the first name that came to mind. He was a great pulp-fiction writer about one-hundred and fifty years ago. He wrote mostly Private Eye stories, but he also took a lark and wrote one Science Fiction work. He titled it The Girl, The Gold Watch, and Everything. I think that I've read everything he ever wrote. So, I call my AI, JD."

Smiling now, Sky asked, "Does he read you to sleep at night?"

Al just looked straight-faced at his friend and said, "Sometimes."

CHAPTER FIVE

14 SEPTEMBER 2116
DINING-IN
USSDF LEYTE GULF

Admiral King and Captain Ward entered the shuttlecraft and were whisked away to the SDF Cruiser, the USSN Leyte Gulf. Before docking with the Cruiser, Admiral King ordered the pilot to take a leisurely tour around the outer hull of this new fighting lady.

Both men were highly impressed with the newest ship in the USSDF Fleet. Following his visual inspection of Leyte Gulf's exterior, Admiral King directed the pilot to commence docking procedures with the SDF Cruiser.

Once the ships were docked, Admiral King and the new Commander of the newly commissioned USSN Astrid, Captain Alan Ward made their way onto the USSN Leyte Gulf. They were met by Captain Jessica Flynn, her Senior Staff, and the Captains of the remaining six ships of the SDF Fleet.

Admiral King's bio had been forwarded to each of the Captains, and though King was well respected for his time in the SDF, his personnel file defused any doubts as to his ability to lead this small fleet, even into combat, if necessary.

Admiral King discovered two things from his private meeting with Captain Flynn. Number one was that the new Cruiser designs were far more spacious than those he had commanded, and two, that Captain Flynn did, indeed, expect him to move his flag to Leyte Gulf. So, after careful consideration, he decided that if things did go south quickly, it would behoove him to command the Fleet from the Leyte Gulf. Also, after some consideration, Admiral Sky King decided that a name was needed for his ten ship Task Force. He wanted a name that would have a special meaning to United States Naval Historians, and after much research, he decided to name it Taffy III, a name dear to the hearts of those who fought the critical World War II naval battle of Leyte Gulf.

560 Days to Earth

14 SEPTEMBER 2116, AD
ON STATION
50,000 MILES PORT SIDE OF HOLLY THORNE

Lieutenant Peter Proud completed the calculations on the progress of Operation Holly Thorne. After checking them three more times, he said, "Computer, where is the XO?"

"The XO is currently on his way to Captain Ward's Ready Room. Would you like for me to contact him?"

"Yes, please."

"Commander Barnes," announced the ship's computer, *"Lieutenant Proud would like to speak with you. Are you available, sir?"*

"Yes, pipe him through," said Commander Darryl Barnes. Barnes had just been promoted to the XO's billet, following Captain Ward's elevation to ship's Captain.

"What'cha got, Pete. I'm on the way to see the Captain, so be quick."

"Yes, sir, of course, sir. Commander, I have just verified that in the two weeks of pushing HT, she has altered position by five degrees to starboard."

"Pete, forward your data to my pad and truck yourself up to the Captain's Ready Room. I'll tell him you are coming. That is wonderful news L T."

"Yes, sir, I'm on my way."

The XO knocked on the Captain's door and was immediately met with, "Come."

The XO entered and was directed to a seat before the Captain's Desk. "Sir," said the XO, my report on ship's readiness is almost green across the board, with one exception; we have a level yellow maintenance warning on the number two R4W cold fusion reactor."

This quickly caught the Captain's attention, and he asked, "You did say yellow on operations, correct?" asked Al Ward.

"Yes, sir, yellow shows it's still running within service parameters, but it is in need of a module replacement. Reactor number two will be down for about two hours. The other R4s are doing fine and can easily carry the load. We'll have it fixed in the next couple of hours."

"All right, as quickly as possible XO, we don't want any further deterioration. A scragged R4, well, you know, just get it done."

"Of course, sir," said the XO.

"Tell me, Daryl, what are the chances of fixing that yellow module?" asked the Captain.

"Captain, with the Maintenance Crew we have aboard, my bet is, it will function better than factory specs by the time the Chief is finished with it."

"Thank you, XO, is there anything else on your mind?"

The XO was about to answer when there was a knock on the Captain's Ready Room door.

"Enter," said the Captain.

The XO said, "Captain, as I was about to say, Lieutenant Proud has some news for you that we believe you will be happy to hear. Mr. Proud," said the XO, as he directed Proud to speak.

"Oh," said the L T, who thought the XO would take credit by telling the Captain, "yes, sir. Captain, as I informed the XO a few moments ago, I can confirm that we have been successful in moving Holly Thorne by five percent of mission goal. Sir, if we can keep up the pressure, we'll be right on time with our estimate of completing the job in ten months."

Captain Ward leaned back in his chair and with a huge smile said, "L T, that is wonderful news. I appreciate your diligence, and I hope you know that I have been interested in you for some time, and I have no doubt your numbers are dead on. Thank you, son, now if you have nothing more for me, you may return to your duties."

As Lieutenant Peter Proud saluted and turned to go, Captain Ward added, "And Proud, download your results to my personal AI, Roger?"

"Yes, of course, Captain. I'll have them to JD in the next ten minutes."

"Fine, Pete, excellent job."

After Proud's departure, the XO smiled at the Captain and said, "Green as grass, and as professional as a ten-year Lieutenant Commander. He will go far whether he remains in the SDF or returns to the Asteroid Mining business. Yes, sir, he'll be a captain in his own right one day. Well, sir, if you have nothing else for me, I'll get back to sticking my nose in the R4 module replacement."

"Very well, Darryl. Don't forget, I'll be at dinner with the Admiral and Captain Flynn. Departure is scheduled for 1600 hours."

"Yes, sir, I'll see you off in Shuttle Bay four at 1600 hours."

And with that, the XO rose from his chair and went back to work.

14 SEPTEMBER 2116
MAINTENANCE AND ENGINEERING SECTION
USSN ASTRID

The CF-BT modules to repair Reactor R4W did indeed prove to be easily swapped out and repaired for potential future use. Master Chief, Kendal (Kit) Karson however, wasn't happy.

Mumbling to himself, he said, "I can't prove it, but I ain't sure this CF-BT module went bad from a factory defect. I can't put my finger on it, but something just don't feel right."

The Master Chief of maintenance and manufacturing aboard Astrid had been working with the R series cold fusion reactors for twenty years. If he felt something wasn't right, well, something was not right.

He called the Chief of the Boat, Senior Master Chief David Harkins and asked him to stop by for a nip.

Storage Bay 4J

14 SEPTEMBER, BAY 4J
USSDF ASTRID

A shadowy figure entered Storage Bay 4J, which held the replacement lasers, along with spare components. Using a counterfeit codex, he was able to enter the locked bay and open the sealed containers without the ship's computers taking notice.

Once inside, he began opening boxes containing the backup lasers. He simply reversed two wires on the first container to be used, which would result in an immediate online failure, plus ten randomly selected lasers stored throughout the Storage Bay. By the simple act of reversing two wires, the saboteur ensured that the laser would burn out within seconds of it being turned on. He then resealed each container. His codex would erase his actions in Bay 4J from the ship's computer database within 30 seconds of resealing the eleventh laser's container.

His original mission had been to simply disrupt the ships ability to efficiently conduct mining operations within the asteroid belt between Mars and Jupiter. Now, however, he knew that his mission had become far more important to the SRI-F.

His computer manipulations left no trace of his act of sabotage, nor would any surveillance mechanism even note his presence in Bay 4J during this clandestine visit. His intent through randomly selected acts of sabotage was to convince Senior Chief Karson that the failures which caused the burnouts resulted from shoddy manufacture at Krupp, Laser Engineering, Gmbh. This would ensure that his mission went undetected.

He left the Bay exactly as he had found it, save for his bit of espionage against the USSDF. It took only ninety minutes to complete his mission and return, unnoticed, to his quarters.

14 SEPTEMBER 2116
MAINTENANCE AND ENGINEERING SECTION
USSN ASTRID

Chief of the Boat, David Harkins entered the Office of Chief Karson and asked, "What's up, Kit, you used our code for possible trouble. Or did you really just want me to drop by for a nip of your Red Eye."

"Yeah," said Chief Karson as he poured Dave a dram of Red Eye. I am concerned about the failure of an R4W replacement module, the CF-BT. In twenty years of dealing with the R4W, and its components, I have never seen a failure quite like this one."

"What are you saying, here, Kit? Do you think we have a saboteur on board?"

"Oh, hell," said Kit, "right now, I just don't know, but what I do know is that this component has been tampered with somewhere along the line. Here, let me put the component under this Spectron-diffuser. Now, look closely at the serial number. Tell me what you see."

"Come on, Kit I'm no mainten…wait, what the hell? Kit, it looks like the last digit of the serial number is scratched. Not much, but when you look closely, it does seem odd. I would say that a screwdriver slipped and raked across the last number."

"Yep," said Kit, "that is exactly what I think did happen."

Now, the Chief of the Boat was intrigued. "Tell me, at what part of the process is the serial number added?"

Kit smiled and said, "See, you're not the Chief of the Boat for nothing. That is exactly what I saw, so I checked and found that the serial numbered plate is the final step in the production process. This number should not be scratched. With the manufacturer's robotic quality control, this could not have been put on with a partially smudged serial number."

"Yeah, I see what you mean, but couldn't this really be something that happened at the factory and just slipped through?"

"I considered that possibility, but when I checked on the procedure at the plant, I just don't see how it could have happened, there. No, Dave, look again, only now look at the weld holding the wiring harness in place. Again, what do you see?"

"The Chief looked closely at the weld and noticed that the minuscule dot of the weld had a touch of slag on its surface."

"Oh, shit, Kit, if all the welds are done at the same time, and cleaned of slag, then this tiny bit could never be there."

"Bingo, this module has been tampered with after it went through quality control. Dave, I can't prove it, but I think that happened after we received the unit."

"Now, hold on," said Dave, "have you checked to see if this module has ever been refurbished by anyone?"

"Yes, I did, and no, it has not. This module was already installed on a brand-new laser when it arrived from the factory."

"Chief, have you checked the computer logs for the R4W in question?"

"Yeah, I did and found nothing out of order. But, Dave, I don't care what the computer logs tell us, this module has been altered to make sure it failed."

"Damn, your case is certainly compelling, but can you prove it? So far, all I've seen is a scratched number and a weld with a small piece of slag still attached to the bead. I ain't sayin' you're wrong, in fact, my money is on you, but you have to admit, it's not much to go on," said the Chief of the Boat.

"Yeah," said Chief Karson, "I know you're right, the evidence is thin and admittedly tiny, but it is not circumstantial. It is there, and it should not be, no, make that, *cannot* be there without manipulation by someone who is very talented. So, Chief of the Boat Harkins, what next?"

"Yes, what indeed? Okay, I believe you are right. We have an enemy aboard. All right, shoot these pictures to my tablet, and I'll take them to the XO. Barnes is a smart guy and has some maintenance background. We'd better include the old man, too.

"Computer, message from Chief Harkins, make an eyes-only for Captain Ward and Commander Barnes, rush an appointment with them from Chief Harkins."

"Chief, the Captain is not currently onboard Astrid. He is aboard the Leyte Gulf for consultation with the Captains of Taffy III. Shall I send your message via his AI?"

"Yes, computer, and notify me as soon as he replies."

"Yes, of course," responded the ship's computer voice.

"Dave," said Chief Kit Karson, "I need to pull the other CF-BT modules from the other eleven R4W reactors; sooner rather than later."

"Yeah, and quietly, too. If we do have a bad boy onboard, we don't want to let him know we suspect espionage."

14 SEPTEMBER 2116
MEETINGS WITH CAPTAINS PUTIN AND CHEN
USSN MINING VESSEL ASTRID

Admiral King spent time reviewing the personnel files of Captains Putin and Chen. What he found in Putin's file demonstrated a deep hatred of the SRI-F, specifically with his native Russia. He felt that the government was far too repressive.

At twenty-two, following his graduation from the Moscow State Mining University as an Asteroid Mining Engineer. He majored in Asteroid Mining, with a minor in Astrogation. Putin then fled his homeland and made his way to Germany, where, he was granted asylum. He was immediately hired as both a Mining Engineer and Assistant Astrogation Specialist, which became his career path.

There appeared to be nothing in Putin's background to suspect he was anything other than what he claimed to be. His career had been steady from day one.

Captain Chen's service record with Asteroid Mining Gmbh also looked very good. He had spent his entire career with the company rising from Mid-shipman to Captain over thirty years in space. There was only one tiny hole in Chen's history. Apparently, he took a leave of absence for one year. During that time there were no entries. He seemed to simply fall off the Earth for one year.

King questioned Chen about this time period, and he stated that he had gone to a Buddhist monastery during this time. Chen said that his family were devout Buddhists and that he had been going through a period of religious crisis. This crisis was resolved after his one-year hiatus.

During one of his daily check-ins with Vice Admiral Perry, Sky asked for an analysis of both Putin and Chen. The result was the same. Sky couldn't seem to shake a kernel of doubt about Chen's monastery story, but he certainly could not prove otherwise.

Admiral King then offered both men the opportunity of remaining in the position of Captain under special contract or transferring to the SRI-F Flagship upon its arrival.

Putin's response was one of utter disdain for the SRI-F and asked to remain as Captain on the Phobos. He also asked about the possibility of being granted a commission in the USSDF.

Chen, however, made no such disclaimers about the SRI-F and informed the Admiral that he would have to consider his options when the SRI-F Fleet arrived.

14 SEPTEMBER 2116
CAPTAIN'S DINING-IN
USSN CRUISER LEYTE GULF

The first formal Dining-In for the Senior Officers of the fleet designated as Taffy III included the Fleet Captains, their XOs, and the Commander of the Marine Detachment, Lieutenant Colonel Patrick Sullivan. Only Captain's Putin and Chen wore the Corporate Uniform of their employer.

With the dinner finished, the Admiral ordered the bottom button of the Officer's Mess White Uniform undone. He then stood and made his way to the podium.

"Ladies and Gentlemen, I wish to express my gratitude for welcoming me, so graciously, into my role as Fleet Commander. Much of yesterday was spent with Captain Flynn going over the sealed orders which she had kept safeguarded for me since departing Red Sands.

"My friends, these orders have radically changed my initial mission parameters. With your arrival, we have gone from a civilian task of moving Holly Thorne's big ass well outside of the orbit of Luna. We are well on the way to accomplishing this undertaking as we are nearly ten percent into the job.

"Now, however, the mission has added a distinct military flavor as I have been informed that the SRI-F has sent a seven-ship fleet on a course to intersect with us around 15 October. There was no direct intimation of hostile intent from the SRI-F in my orders, but those orders did say that the SRI-F vessels were equipped with rail guns and nuclear missiles.

"We are now tasked with preventing the SRI-F from firing those missiles into our comet, until, or unless, we have proven incapable of completing our primary assignment. Getting down to the nitty-gritty; we are cleared to use force to prevent the SRI-F from prematurely launching their nukes."

Several Captains looked a bit surprised as they realized that using force against the SRI-F Fleet meant global war on Earth, and global war was unthinkable.

King informed his officers of the sealed orders he had received from Captain Flynn. He also made the official announcement that he would be moving his flag to the Leyte Gulf sometime in the next forty-eight hours. As he returned to his seat following his speech and the inevitable questions, Admiral King offered the final toast of the evening.

"Ladies and Gentlemen, a final toast, if you please; to absent comrades." This traditional toast was offered to honor those who sacrificed their lives in service to their country.

Captain Ward was seated to the right of Admiral Sky King. After hearing his AI's message from Chief of the Boat Harkins, he discretely passed the message on to Admiral King via AI. The Admiral asked if Ward knew what the Chief could possibly want.

"No, sir, I don't, but it must be of some import if Chief Harkins has sent this message to me. I am more concerned that he sent the message, eyes only, and did not elaborate on the reason."

"All right," said Sky, "send a message to the ship's computer telling the Chief that we would like to speak to him concerning information garnered by our meetings. Let him know we will return to the ship at around 2330 hours. I'll break this shindig up in another hour."

15 SEPTEMBER 2116
CAPTAIN'S READY ROOM
USSN ASTRID

Admiral King decided to put off the meeting with Chief of the Boat Harkins until 0800 hours of 15 September. The meeting consisted of Admiral King, Captain Ward, Commander Barnes, Senior Master Chief Harkins, Master Chief Karson, and Vice Admiral Perry, via AI. His presence was not disclosed to the other attendees.

The ship's computer was ordered not to record this meeting. Both Admiral's AIs would, however, make verbatim recordings of the proceedings.

Chief Karson laid out his concerns about possible espionage and was supported by Chief Harkins. The physical evidence was displayed leaving little doubt in the Officer's minds that they did, indeed, have a destructive force aboard the Astrid.

Admiral King ordered the replacement and inspection of all CF-BT modules aboard the Astrid. Inspecting the CF-BT modules on the Phobos and Ceres seemed unwise as this action may alert the saboteur that his acts of sabotage had been uncovered.

Following the meeting, the two Admirals discussed possible available avenues to snare the spy. Admiral King ordered his AI to download all computer files concerning the damaged R4W reactor. The two men hoped that the computer specialists at NASA could find some evidence of tampering with the video files. Beyond that, there seemed little else to do.

King wanted to bring Captain Ward into the loop concerning the AI communications breakthrough and the Thirty-Eight Protocol.

Vice Admiral Perry denied Sky's request, stating that, until the mystery was solved, everyone on Astrid was under some level of suspicion.

15 SEPTEMBER 2116, AD 1800 HOURS
ON STATION
50,000 MILES PORTSIDE OF HOLLY THORNE

Admiral King's AI, JJ, informed Sky that the time for a commo check with Vice Admiral Perry was due in one minute, 1800 hours.

"Thanks, JJ," said Sky, make contact and then I'll speak with the Admiral."

At exactly 1800 hours the commo check between AIs was completed, and the Vice Admiral's AI was informed that Admiral King wished to speak with him. Dolph came on line a second later saying, "Hello, Sky, what's new?"

"Dolph, I just wanted to personally report that Operation HT is progressing exactly as planned. We have now been utilizing our lasers for two weeks, and Holly Thorne's trajectory has been moved by five percent of goal."

"Sky, that is, indeed, wonderful news. Say, how do you keep those lasers from overheating and blowing out? You do have replacements, I presume?"

"Yes, sir, we run the lasers on a rotation between the three ships. They are, however not on constant burn. The lasers fire in accordance with the rotation of Holly Thorne. This allows for relatively short bursts in the same place as she turns over.

"Two ships are firing all the time while one rests. We do the same with our individual onboard lasers. Only two-thirds of them operate at any given time. And yes, we do have five replacements for each laser."

CHAPTER SIX

559 Days to Earth

15 SEPTEMBER 2116, AD
PHILADELPHIA, PA

Roger Dean, one of General Wolfe's Aides, buzzed the General's desk,

"Yes," said General Wolfe.

"Sir, it's Roger Dean, I think you should turn on CNN. There's trouble in Philly."

Wolfe said to his AI, "Give me a CNN Newsfeed."

Immediately the COS was able to see the newscast on what appeared to be a seventy-five-inch video screen. He watched as the Philadelphia Affiliate of CNN announced that a large protest march, apparently organized by Pastor Elijah Wright's Church of the Light.

The affiliate reporter said, "The Pastor, himself is not available for comment, but a Senior Deacon of the Church has a statement to read. Please, go ahead, Deacon."

The Deacon thanked the reporter and made it clear that this gathering was no protest march, but the beginning of a movement which will save the world from destruction.

He then read the following statement. *"Peoples of the world, we are here in Philadelphia, the City of Brotherly Love to announce that the Messiah has returned to walk among us. Our Pastor, Elijah Wright, has been taken by a host of heavenly Angels to his just reward, and the Lord and Savior, the Child of God, the Host of Hosts has taken his body. Yeshua lives and will make his presence known to all, tomorrow at 1:00 pm.*

"His words will echo throughout the world, proclaiming His return. He returns, not as a Prince of Peace, but as the Warrior Prince proclaimed in the Book of Revelations. On these streets, you see a peaceful demonstration of nearly ten-thousand saved souls. On this day there will be no rioting, no harsh words, threats, or demands, but know Ye that the Warrior Prince, the Son of God will speak from our Church of the Light to tell the world of God's plan to give mankind one final chance at redemption. The Church only holds six-thousand worshippers. Speakers will be set up around the Plaza fronting The Church of the Light. JESUS IS AGAIN AMONG US! HALLELUJAH!"

The CNN Reporter said, "So, there you have it. Once again Philadelphia is to become the center for revolution. Reverend Wright, the self-proclaimed Son of God, Jesus Christ will speak to the world tomorrow at 1:00 pm. Tune in to CNN for the latest on this developing story.

15 SEPTEMBER 2116, 1:00 PM
CHURCH OF THE LIGHT
PHILADELPHIA, PA

Had there not been ten-thousand parishioners in the streets, the announcement of a news conference would have been cause for laughter. However, just as Pastor Wright, aka Yeshua, anticipated, the news networks were all in attendance. They were set up and ready for his pronouncements.

CNN reporter Adrian Brandt, in a soft voice, said, "The huge crowd gathered in and outside of the Church of the Light must number near one-hundred thousand, and I am receiving reports that thousands more are taking to the streets to be a part of this spectacle.

"At this moment, Reverend Wright, who claims to be Jesus Christ, the Son of God is seated to the right of the pulpit from which he will make his statement. Surprisingly, this crowd is calm, quiet, and eagerly waits to hear what the Pastor has to say.

As the comet Holly Thorne approaches, many feel that the return of Jesus is to be expected. Oh, look, Reverend Wright is standing and making his way to the pulpit. Reverend Wright, who many say is just another false prophet while others believe that he is the embodiment of the Son of God."

His parishioners watched in a state of rapture as the Reverend rose from his chair and walked slowly to his Pulpit. As he dramatically raised his head in a slow and scripted manner, the Pastor's eyes took on the barest hint of a golden sheen. His face also appeared to hint of gold. He looked out over the multitudes numbering perhaps as many as fifty-thousand filled the Church and many streets.

He raised his hands into the air, allowing the purple of his vestments to be clearly seen. The crowd immediately quieted and waited for their Messiah to speak.

His address began in a conversational tone, but quickly rose, as did his passion, he said, "Hallelujah! Salvation and glory and power belong to the One True God, Jehovah. For His judgments are true and just; for He has judged the great prostitutes, that are the sinful governments of Man. For they have corrupted the earth with their immorality, and have poured upon her the blood of His servants."

Once more they cried out, HALLELUJAH!

He continued; "The smoke from THE PURGING OF THE SINS OF MAN GOES UP FOREVER AND EVER! BEHOLD! THE FINGER OF GOD APPROACHES. GOD HAS GIVEN YOU ONE FINAL CHANCE TO REPENT YOUR SINS, AND CLEANSE THE EARTH OF THE VILE GOVERNMENTS, RUN BY IMMORAL, CORRUPT, AND SINFUL MEN WHO LUST AFTER POWER OVER THE MULTITUDES."

His voice then dropped from passion to an earnest, heartfelt plea, "You must take heed, and accept the love of God before it is too late. Praise God! Jehovah has thrown a dirty snowball at you, and you must change your ways. You must become the People of God! You must stop worshipping at the altar of lust!

"When my Father gave you this planet, it was a paradise, now, it is a cesspool of filth, greed, lust, and degradation of every sort. I say to you that I have been sent to judge the people of this Earth. I have not come as the Prince of Peace, but rather as a Judge. I, alone, will decide if Man is worthy of receiving God's Grace. I warn you, take heed, for if you fail in your God's demand, his simple snowball will not miss the Earth, but will destroy it.

"Even now, you have sent mere men to push the comet of God away from the Earth. THIS IS BLASPHEMY! For should you fail in God's last test, He shall return his tool of destruction to collide with you. REPENT! REPENT, NOW! Over the next two months, here in the United States, elections will be held to determine who shall rule in this nation. Good Men of Faith are being chosen to run for these offices. Yes, this is the first part of God's test for Man.

"Once the government of the United States is in the hands of God's chosen few, other nations will follow until your world is united under the One True God, Jehovah. The path is clear, and it is yours for the taking. You must choose. Do not fail to act, time is short, JUDGEMENT DAY IS AT HAND!"

And with that, the new Messiah turned away from his audience and walked off the stage. Those in attendance fell to their knees praying for salvation. The streets, filled with thousands, were also silent as they prayed.

"Oh crap!" said the President's Chief of Staff. He redialed Roger Dean and directed him to put together a file on this Pastor Wright and pass it along to the General's AI.

He then sent a transcript of the statement, which was garnered by his AI, and forwarded it to the President, along with a request to meet with her, ASAP.

16 SEPTEMBER 2116,
OFFICE OF THE SUPREME LEADER
TEHRAN, IRAN

"The Great Satan is again insulting Islam." A member of the Ruling Mullahs informed the Supreme Leader of Iran. "In Philadelphia, a man claims to be the resurrected Jesus Christ. He calls on all nations of the

Earth to deny Islam and to become Christian in order to save Earth from destruction by the comet which bears down upon us.

"Supreme Leader, surely this outrage cannot go unpunished. I urge you to pronounce a Fatwa against this blasphemer of the one true God, Allah, Allahu Akbar."

"No, my friend," said the Supreme Leader, "there shall be no Fatwa. I agree that this false prophet must die, but we must do this quietly, and with no trail leading back to us. I task you with making contact with the Special Operations Branch within the QUDS Force. Pass this mission to them with my approval and remind them to use discretion. He must arrange it so that the hated Zionists appear responsible. Allahu Akbar!"

And with that, the Iranian Cleric was excused to contact the QUDS Force Commander, Major General Mohammad Kasemadi.

16 SEPTEMBER 2116, AD
OVAL OFFICE WHITE HOUSE
WASHINGTON, DC

Tessa, the President's Secretary ushered the "Comet Committee", as they had named themselves, into the Conference Room. Once everyone was seated, the President, Mrs. Eileen N. Greene entered. As the attendees began to rise, Eileen directed them to remain in their seats. This habit of Presidential informality was a constant irritant to the ultra-formal Chief of Staff.

The President began with her COS, "Harry, please give us your thoughts on the Right Reverend Wright, aka Jesus Christ."

"Yes, Madame President, the Reverend has a long history of long rants in which he rails against the immorality of the government, specifically, the White Government. In the past, his antics have been almost comedic, but now we might have a problem."

"How so?" asked Eileen.

The COS leveled his gaze at the President before replying. He said, "Madame President, he has touched a nerve with huge numbers of the electorate. As Holly Thorne becomes visible, people will become scared. This will be as a direct result of his constant barrage against the corrupt, and immoral, government.

"Ma'am, it is quite possible that a groundswell of fear could sweep the Reverend's candidates into office, giving him virtual control of the purse strings of our Republic."

Eileen looked shocked as she replied, "Harry, do you believe this scenario is a real possibility?"

"Madame President, I believe it is far more than a possibility. Holly will arrive just before the mid-term electees take office. More and more voters will begin to wonder if Wright's words really do come from God. They will be seeking redemption and God's grace. So, yes ma'am, this could well be our future."

Turning to the National Chief of Intelligence, the President asked, "George, what are your findings?"

"Madame President, I must concur with the assessment of the Chief of Staff. We are entering uncharted waters. Imagine, if you will, a newly installed Legislative Branch filled with the followers of a Religious Zealot like Wright.

"The early information we are receiving around the world is that if the US goes with Wright, many other nations will follow. The nations embracing Islam, however, will resist this movement and may declare war on Israel.

"Ma'am, the potential for disaster will increase exponentially over the next month, leading up to the elections. The timing for Wright is absolutely stellar. People will feel compelled to act, with little time for reflection as they perceive desperate times hurling at them."

"Wow!" said a shaken President of the United States. "Perceiving the logic of your arguments, I have to ask; what do we do about this?"

The intelligence chief said, "Madame President, I would ask that you keep a tight rein on Israel. If the Mossad assassinates him and word gets out, well, I can see the headlines now; Jewish Pharisees have murdered Christ for the second time. Our position in support of Israel would become untenable.

"I do have one huge concern that Iran may assassinate Wright and leave evidence of a Mossad Hit. The result is the same and is a powder-keg. Where ever Wright goes he must be tailed by unobtrusive security. If he is, in fact, assassinated, a Clean-up Team must be close by to remove any evidence left behind and replace it with evidence of an Iranian Hit."

"So," said the President, "we must protect Wright and lose control of the government or stand back and just wait for him to be assassinated, with the blame falling on Israel. Will someone please offer another solution, because what we have on the table is totally unsatisfactory."

"Yes, ma'am," said Homeland Security, "Madame President, I am most reticent to suggest this, but we must consider assassinating him ourselves and blaming the Iranians. No matter how you slice it, we are coming close to war for the first time in fifty years. Still, we must consider this option."

Every member of this committee felt immense relief because they were thinking the exact same thing. President Greene looked individually at each person at the table before saying, "Yes, reticent or not, this option must be considered."

The COS said, "Perhaps, Madame President, there is another way. I believe we should consider delaying the Mid-Term Elections until after Holly Thorne passes. In this scenario, if Holly fails to create a pandemic, then elections happen immediately upon her passing. If she does infect the world, then I don't see how any of this even matters. Our main objective here is to avoid a war which, I believe, would lead to a scorched and uninhabitable world."

"Harry, the fallout will be welcomed by the Legislature incumbents and hated by Wright and his followers. I like your idea, good thinking. Gentlemen, this is the path we take. I will announce the delayed elections two days before. Let's get the talking heads and the incumbents announcing their idea of delaying elections until after the comet's passing."

17 SEPTEMBER 2116, AD 1200 HOURS
ON STATION
50,000 MILES PORTSIDE OF HOLLY THORNE

"Sir," said JJ, *"I have an important connection from Vice Admiral Perry."*

"Thank you, JJ. Yes, sir, go ahead."

"Admiral," said Perry in a formal tone, "things have taken several dangerous turns here. I'm sending downloads to your AI to give you a heads up. Check them out immediately. Look them over. Every option discussed is dicey at best. Anyway, let's chat again at 1800: Perry, out."

20 SEPTEMBER 2116, AD 1000 HOURS
FOX NEWS
NEW YORK BUREAU

At the FOX News Network 10:00 a.m. news hour the Anchor Desk began with a report that a bi-partisan move from both sides of the Congressional Isle was floating the idea of postponing the Mid-Term Elections until ten days after the Holly Thorne Comet has safely passed the Earth.

"This bi-partisan effort they say, will allay the concerns of the voters and allow things to calm down as the comet's approach is adding far too much, "what if" confusion into the election process."

"By delaying the election, the American voters will have sufficient time to assess the best path for the United States without the deafening roar caused by the passage of Holly Thorne," said Herman Marshall, Democratic Congressman from New York."

The News Anchor continued saying that this move might create much more confusion and concern, in that the United States has never before taken such a step to delay the vote.

He added that the Reverend Wright, aka, Jesus Christ, has promised a legal challenge to prevent such a move. He also shared his concerns that riots would likely erupt across the country, leading to massive damage to the inner-cities and major loss of life.

The News Anchor said, "I would think it would be much simpler for the Reverend, in his role of Jesus Christ, Superstar, to simply utilize his powers as God to create a miracle for all to witness that would be sufficient to solve this disaster. Instead, it appears that he has just added fuel to an already raging fire."

Coinciding with the FOX News Report, CNN's headline for the same time slot led with the banner, the Conservative Constitutionalist Party, the CCP, intends to end the electoral process in America.

The Anchor stated, "This move, is undoubtedly designed to seize the nation in the vice of a Dictatorial Government controlled by a Military Junta. Such action from the CCP will most certainly cause this nation to dissolve into Anarchy and Civil War.

"With this latest attempted power-grab, it becomes apparent that the CCP President, Eileen Greene does not have the necessary skillset to save our Republic. May God have mercy on us all."

Within an hour of the CNN post, the streets came alive with protest, riots, and looting. Fires were set, overwhelming the Fire Departments. What many thought would ignite a Civil War in America quickly deteriorated into another episode of the destruction of the inner-cities through burning and looting.

The President called in the National Guard to bolster the Police. In Chicago, this move only resulted in inciting the rioters to greater acts of violence when gunfire erupted from windows above the streets. Seven Police Officers and four Guardsman were killed in the first volley. The National Guard returned fire causing the protestors to begin stampeding through the streets. Throughout the night, sporadic vehicles were set ablaze as snipers began the hit and run game which turned the streets of several major cities into war zones.

21 SEPTEMBER 2116, AD 1200 HOURS
OVAL OFFICE, WHITE HOUSE
WASHINGTON, DC

The Comet Committee, along with the Joint Chiefs of the Military met in the President's Conference Room. President Eileen N. Greene looked sad and worn as she gaveled the conference into session.

"Gentlemen, our plan to ease past the emotion of Holly Thorne's passing seems to have backfired. Perhaps that CNN moron was right in that, I may not have the necessary skillset to right this ship, but the people in this room do. So, what do we do?"

The COS said, "It seems, to me, that Wright was one step ahead of us on this one. Apparently, his followers were patiently waiting for us to make just this exact move."

The Chairman of the Military Joint Chiefs of Staff asked to speak, "Madame President, unless we take immediate action this rebellion will soon gain a momentum that could, in fact, cause the collapse of the United States. It is the considered opinion of the Joint Chiefs that you immediately order the military into the streets to quell this uprising. Lives will be lost, but the Republic will be saved."

Homeland Security said, "Madame President, if we utilize our military to regain control, we will have certainly left the Constitution in tatters. While the premise of this move is to preserve the Union, we will have also set a precedent for some future President to do exactly what CNN has just accused us of doing.

21 SEPTEMBER 2116, AD 10:00 A.M.
ENTRANCE TO THE CHURCH OF THE LIGHT
PHILADELPHIA, PA

Reverend Wright announced that at 10:00 a.m., he would stop the uprisings that had been raging since the CNN report of Civil War in

America. The Media frenzy to record this miracle promised by Wright managed to be online and ready for him to provide evidence of his god-like power.

At precisely 10:00 a.m., the Reverend exited the Church building and stood before the throngs of people and Media Crews. Across America, the riots abruptly stopped as those protesting looked to their cell phones to hear what their Jesus was about to say.

Wright stood quietly until the crowds were silent and attentive before saying, "People of Earth, watch and believe." He then raised both arms toward the heavens. After two seconds, he lowered his hands, turned and calmly walked back into the Chapel.

The Media was stunned and felt short-changed. What had happened, nothing. Yet, within seconds, reports began to come in stating that the riots within the largest cities in America had ceased, and the protestors had simply stopped and walked back to their homes.

Inside the Sanctuary, again alone with his inner-circle, Wright and company laughed heartily. "Well," said Wright, "the Block Captains have done very well in keeping our supporters in line. When I raised my arms in supplication, I actually felt like I was Jesus. Who knows? Maybe I am. Maurice, make sure the organizers receive a 'well done' from me."

"Yes, my Lord," laughed Maurice, "will do, *for thine is the power*."

Tens of millions of Americans were taken in by the machinations of Wright and now believed that he was, in fact, the embodiment of Christ. Good planning, a compliant Media, and magnificent choreography had elevated Wright to Jesus Christ.

21 SEPTEMBER 2116, AD 1015 HOURS
PRESIDENT'S CONFERENCE ROOM
WASHINGTON, DC

"All right," said President Greene, "how did he pull off his *miracle*?"

The COS said, "Good planning, a compliant Media, and simple theatrics. All happening at this critical time in our world's history. Madame President, Wright has proven to be an excellent planner and showman.

"I do not believe that we can now stop him from pulling off this charade to take control of our Republic. We can no longer delay the elections unless we really do want bloodshed across the US. So, unless we can find a way to get Wright to back off, his candidates will likely be swept into office.

"Ma'am, I recommend that you invite the new Jesus to the White House. In private we can make him realize that he's full of shit. We put it to him, plain and simple, work with us to maintain the nation, or never be heard from again. If he balks and actually claims to be Jesus, then put a pitcher of water on the desk and demand he turns it into wine.

"Then, I believe it to be best if you hold a televised chat with the nation, reassuring the citizenry that elections will take place on time. Let the people know that the idea of delaying the vote was just that, an idea expressed by several members of Congress.

"You must also ask for calm and suggest that Americans are not fooled by parlor tricks." Discussion around the table was passionate but eventually came to accept the perspective of the COS.

Following his meeting with the President, Wright agreed to play ball. His popularity continued to rise among his followers to the godlike stature he so fervently sought. The President held a fireside chat with America centered on Reverend Wright's visit to the White House. This helped to calm the nation and lower tensions.

CHAPTER SEVEN

Late September in Washington seemed to herald the approach of Fall and the changing colors of the trees. The daytime temperatures were still quite warm but dropped a bit more each night.

The Chief of Staff, retired Lieutenant General Harry Wolfe and the NASA Chief, Gordon Winters arrived for the scheduled briefing of the President on the progress of Holly Thorne.

President Greene asked Tess to show the two men in. Tess also provided a carafe of fresh coffee. Once the two briefers were seated, the President said, "All right, Harry, cough it up. Is the plan working?"

Harry deferred to NASA who smiled broadly and said, "Madame President, we have just been informed by Admiral Perry that on 18 September, following two weeks of being nudged by Admiral King's mining vessels, the comet had moved five percent of mission goals."

Eileen looked at both men and asked, "Okay, five percent; is that good?" Please continue, Gordon."

"Oh, yes ma'am, five percent is the exact number we were hoping for. Barring any missteps, Holly Thorne will be moved to mission goals at the end of the ten-month operation."

"Missteps, what kind of missteps? Maintenance should not be problematic. They have spares, don't they?"

"Madame President," interrupted the COS, "that far out in space, anything could happen. We just don't even know all the possibilities for missteps that might be out there to derail this operation. Personally, my biggest fear is the SRI-F's potential for interference."

"Yes, I see," said Eileen Greene, "you are, of course, right to add a disclaimer to the briefing, especially where the SRI-F is concerned. I can't say I'm overconfident that the SRI-F will refrain from using Holly as target practice. Oh, they promised not to interfere as long as the operation is progressing according to plan, but trust them? Not bloody likely."

24 SEPTEMBER 2116, AD
JFK INTERNATIONAL AIRPORT
NEW YORK, NY

Salmon Dudayev, a Caucasian, from Chechnya arrived at JFK International Airport on a Lufthansa flight originating in Frankfurt, Germany. He was traveling under the name of Simon Drucker. His passport stated that he was a German national, born in Dusseldorf, Germany on January 5, 2096.

There actually was a Simon Drucker who looked much like Dudayev. His body had been fed into a wood chipper and fed to monkeys.

Salmon Dudayev looked positively European, complete with sandy-blonde hair and blue eyes. His passport stated he was Jewish, he was, in fact, a devout Muslim, and he intended to become a martyr for Allah. There was nothing in Simon Drucker's past to raise any concern. He had been a young, up and coming Pharmaceutical Representative for Bayer Gmbh.

He passed through customs without a hitch and after renting a Cadillac from Hertz made his way to Philadelphia. Upon his arrival at the Hilton Philadelphia at Penn's Landing. Dudayev's bags were unloaded by a Bellman who patiently waited until Dudayev/Drucker had turned his car over to the Parking Valet Service Worker.

The Bellman then led the way to the Guest Check-in Counter. His reservation requirements were for a quiet room overlooking the river yet far away from the elevators and vending machines.

The following morning, Simon Drucker took a private, limo driven tour of the city, which now included The Church of the Light, headquarters of the returned Christ.

Drucker took copious photos and videos of each stop, though his only true interest was in The Church of the Light.

At 2:00 p.m. Simon Drucker arrived at the Deutsche Bank at 1735 Market Street where a safe deposit box had been opened for him by another Rep of Bayer Gmbh.

Once Simon was in a private cubicle, he opened the large box and found a lightweight vest with four straps of Semtex plastic explosives, and one dead-man's switch with the proper connections. Additionally, the box held $10,000, one Beretta Model 71 LRS, chambered in .22 LR with three magazines loaded with hollow points, one Sig Sauer 228, chambered in 9 mm, three magazines loaded with hollow point ammunition. These weapons were over one hundred and fifty years old, which made for easy identification.

The Beretta Model 71 was the favorite handgun of the Israeli Mossad. It would be left at the scene of Wright's murder.

The plan, simple, yet bold, was to be near the front pews. During a prayer, Drucker would quickly rise and fire his Sig 9 mm into the body and head of Wright. He would then turn the weapon upon himself and fire a 9 mm round into his mouth. The shock of the shot would cause the assassin to release the dead man's switch causing a loud and devastating explosion. The shot to the face would destroy the ability to properly identify the body as anyone other than Simon Drucker, even if any identification was possible.

The attack was planned for Sunday's 08:00 a.m. Service on September 27th.

27 SEPTEMBER 2116, AD 0600 HOURS
THE CHURCH OF THE LIGHT
PHILADELPHIA, PA

Anticipating a long line, Drucker arrived at the Church at 6:00 a.m. He was stunned to see thousands already in line for the 8:00 Service. Drucker quickly realized he needed a new plan. Seeing this throng of worshipers, he realized that it was highly unlikely that he would even be able to get into the 10:00 Service. He, therefore, decided to find another way to get access to Wright.

Drucker returned to his hotel room and began looking for apartment rentals fronting The Church of the light. He was somewhat surprised to find that there were several units available for a one-year lease.

He called the Apartment Finder Office and spoke with a Realtor. She informed him that all the commotion, noise, and night lights had sent many residents to more quiet apartments away from the hoopla.

Following the signing of the lease and taking possession of the unit, Drucker placed a personal ad in the local Internet Gay Connections Guide for Philadelphia. The ad read:

SWGM seeks SBGM as partner for a new experience with holographic audience. Respond via Box 4269, this publication. I'm excited to meet you, you rascal.

This posting was his way to contact his handler for support, and information explaining why the original mission would be scrapped.

SWGM was normally meant to be Single White Gay Man, Drucker, and SBGM coded as Single Black Gay Man, Wright. The reference to a holographic audience meant he needed a holographic projector. Excited to meet you meant, no contact, use the Deutsche Bank Deposit Box, and you rascal meant that he was unable to carry out the attack as planned.

There were several responses to his original ad, but only one caught his eye, the ad read, "Hi Slim, word is you need a long dong, I'll meet you at the ICandy Bar at .254 S. 12th Street. Just let me know what time and how to recognize you."

The code name for Drucker was Slim. The coded message told him that his new toys would be in the Bank Box. The number 25, as in the Street number was only part of the date. To properly read the day of delivery Drucker's handler had to add the numbers 1+2, from 12th Street, to the 25, meaning that the projector would be available on the 28th. The term long dong meant that he would also find a collapsible 7 mm sniper rifle in the box.

On the afternoon of the 28th Drucker retrieved his tools from the Bank Box. He placed the items in his sedan and drove to an abandoned quarry in Delaware to zero in his new toy. His rifle, unlike his sidearms, was not an antique, but rather a state of the art, bolt action, massively powered air-shot, made in Israel.

There was little noise and the dart fired was a 7 mm discarding sabot round traveling at a velocity of five-thousand two-hundred feet per second. It really didn't matter where the dart hit his target, the kinetic energy expended upon contact would turn any human target into soup. A bullet-proof vest meant nothing to Drucker's discarding sabot round.

The holo-projector would project the image at the shooter's window position of closed curtains to prevent counter snipers from seeing Drucker's position. It was like an old one-way mirror.

Following the shot, Drucker would clean his fingerprints, then quietly leave the apartment. He would return home the following week from Miami International Airport to Frankfurt. The Beretta and the Sniper Rifle would be left in the Apartment.

28 SEPTEMBER 2116, AD
ON STATION
50,000 MILES PORTSIDE OF HOLLY THORNE

An explosion rocked the number one mining laser just after the temperature gauge suddenly flared to red. The laser blister mounted on the outer hull of Astrid did contain the blast but left the containment area a smoking ruin.

Chief Karson and his damage control team quickly shut down all power to the laser compartment and began an inspection of the extensive damage. Fortunately, the laser blisters were unmanned. The crew and computer overwatch of the systems were located in a segregated area of the Maintenance compartments on J Deck, midship.

Chief of the Boat Harkins rushed to the Laser Blister to get a sitrep from Karson. "Chief," asked Harkins, "what's the bottom line on the damage?"

Karson's face showed a faint gray outline around his face, from the smoke as he took off his breather. "Well, as you can see, the laser is a total write off. Clean up, and replacement will take about eight hours before we can get back on-line. Right now, I don't have any idea why this happened. Suspicions yes, but beyond that, no clue.

"Tell the Skipper that I can't begin to figure out what happened until the replacement laser has been inspected and is up and running. Dave, at this point I just don't trust anyone, so I'll have to oversee the inspection and installation personally."

"Thanks, Kit, what say I drop by in about ten hours. Which maintenance bay are you planning to use?"

"I'll be in Bay 8, here on J Deck, it's the closest. Tell me, Chief, have you ever even heard of this happening to a mining laser?"

"No, Kit, I have not. Look, I've gotta run and tell the Old Man how things are progressing. I'll see you later."

30 SEPTEMBER 2116, AD
3RD FLOOR APARTMENT
1,129 YARDS TO CHURCH DOOR

At 8:17 p.m. the crowded streets fronting The Church of the Light began to buzz in anticipation of Wright's appearance at the door to say goodnight to the multitudes.

At 8:20 p.m. the doors opened, and a dozen bodyguards exited the Church clearing a path for the Son of God. The guards formed a loose barricade around Wright with just enough space for him to appear to his followers.

Drucker was pleased that his moment of glory for Allah had finally arrived. The sight picture was centered on Wright's chest as Drucker took a deep breath, then released half, and slowly squeezing the trigger with the pad of his right index finger until the weapon discharged its dart in a whoosh. The assassin mentally shouted Praise Allah, Allahu Akbar!

The miniature 7 mm sabot round, traveling at nearly one mile per second struck Wright squarely in the chest before Drucker could remove his finger from the trigger.

Pandemonium erupted in the streets as Wright was literally blown into pieces from the kinetic energy being released as the round passed through his chest. Passing straight through Drucker's target the round struck the brick wall immediately behind him. A large portion of the wall shattered into thousands of deadly brick pieces of shrapnel, killing all of Wright's guards and wounding twenty others.

Drucker then calmly left the apartment and made his way to the street where he took on the persona of those in the panicked crowd who fled helter-skelter away from The Church of the Light. He was soon lost in the stampede. Within an hour he found himself safely away. He returned to his hotel and upon entering his room, opened the mini-fridge for a snack and turned on FOX News.

The US and much of the world erupted in a berserker rage which took many hundreds of lives and caused billions of dollars in damages.

Only in the Muslim communities of the world was there joy and celebration at the death of who, they called, The Satanic-Christ. This brought on a Christian backlash against Muslim communities around the world which left more than twenty-five thousand dead on both sides.

Upon discovering the shooter's nest, an FBI Clean-up Team was dispatched to investigate. Anything relating to Israel was removed and replaced. In their place weapons and explosives with ties to Iran were found. A well-read and tattered Quran, printed in Farsi, the official language of Iran was also left behind.

Ninety-six hours later, Drucker/Dudayev was back in Chechnya where he was met and welcomed as a hero just before he was shot. There would be no loose ends.

CHAPTER EIGHT

542 Days to Earth

28 SEPTEMBER 2116, AD
ON STATION
50,000 MILES PORTSIDE OF HOLLY THORNE

The midnight oil was burning in Bay 8, J Deck as Master Chief Kit Karson diligently worked to unravel the mystery of what caused an unprecedented super-spike explosion of the Number one mining laser.

The Chief of the Boat came into Bay 8 with a fresh pot of coffee and sandwiches.

"Okay, Kit, you got anything yet?"

"Yeah, Chief, I do, but again it is only a tiny bit of evidence. Our saboteur is damned good. Then, again, so am I, so now it's become a competition of who is better. Dave, see if you can get a meetup with the Skipper. I think I need to personally let him know what I've found."

"Computer," said Chief Harkins, "send a message to the Captain requesting a meeting with myself and Master Chief Karson."

"Yes, Chief," replied the computer's friendly voice. "I have sent your request, and I will get back to you as soon as he replies. Oh, wait, the Captain has just sent a reply that he will come to your location in about ten minutes."

"Tell the Skipper we'll be in Bay 8, J Deck."

"Done," replied the computer.

Smiling now, Chief Harkins said, "Wow, the Old Man is on his way to you. I'm impressed."

"Shut up, Dave, he just wants to see the damage for himself."

"Yeah, well, I'm just sayin'. Now show me what you've got, so far."

"Hey, relax for a second, will ya? I don't want to go over this twice in ten minutes. I will tell you this, however…"

But before Chief Karson could finish his sentence, the XO, Commander Barnes entered the bay and said, "The Captain is on the way. He's maybe two minutes behind me. Holy shit! What a mess. Chief, I've been in asteroid mining for 15 years, and I have never seen an accident like this, wow."

The XO and the Chief of the Boat both began wandering around the damaged laser, while they waited for the Captain.

The Skipper arrived two minutes later and whistled, "Damn, Chief, what did you do?"

Karson took the Captain as serious and getting his back up, said, "Now, sir, I resent any implication that I…"

"Whoa, Kit," said the Captain, "I was only kidding. I know you're not responsible for this disaster. Okay? We good?"

Kit realized that he had crossed over a line that he was sure must be quickly recrossed, he apologized and said, "Sir, I didn't mean to snap at you, it's just that this day has been exhausting, but sir, now I can prove that we have a saboteur aboard. Catching him is your department, but I can show you his handiwork." The old Master Chief said, "Cap'n, this guy is good, really good, but I'm better."

"I agree that you are the best Chief of Maintenance and Machining that I have ever known, but do you think you might get on with it?" asked Captain Ward.

"Yes, sir, of course, but dang it, I found him out. Now, sir, once I began goin' through the personnel records to check on qualifications, I sorted the skills necessary to do the sabotage and cover his tracks with the computer. Well, I discovered that there is only one man on this ship that seems to have all the skills necessary to single-handedly pull this off.

"Of course, if there's more than one bad guy involved, then there are several fits, but just one has all the skills," exclaimed a now exuberant Chief Karson.

Fighting frustration, the Chief of the Boat said, "Damn it, Karson, who the hell is it? Come on, spit it out, ya old fart."

Not wanting to get his old friend, Dave Harkins mad at him, Karson said, "Okay, okay, our saboteur is our new Payload Master, Chief Jay Donovon. Hey, I just realized something else."

"What's that Chief?" asked the XO.

"I guess finding our bad boy isn't just your area after all."

The XO couldn't help but smile as he said, "Yes, Chief, you are a regular Sherlock Holmes. Okay, now I want both of you to keep quiet about this. I don't want Donovon to know we're on to him. Oh, wait, one more thing Chief, what did you find that made you know this mess was sabotage, as opposed to a simple malfunction?"

"Well, thank you for askin', sir. I was beginnin' to think that you weren't goin' to ask.

"Okay, okay," Chief Harkins, "I'm gettin' to it. Sir, the tip-off was staring me in the face for hours before I figured it out. Dave, stop lookin' at me like that. I have to tell this in my own way, so you just relax and listen, Roger?"

"Yeah, yeah, Roger, so go ahead, get on with it."

"Yes," said XO Barnes, I am anxious to do some research on Donovon, myself."

"Okay, I get it. So, I was pickin' over every inch of this burned up crap when I finally spotted it. The remains of two wires had been reversed, and no, it was not done at the factory. This had to be done here, during the last laser rest period. As soon as this baby was fired up, she immediately flared and caused the explosion."

"What about the other lasers that are online? Are they in danger of exploding?"

"Oh, no, sir," said Chief Karson, "if their wires were reversed, they would have gone up just like old number one here."

"Well, that's a relief. So, you're saying we're good to go on the other lasers, right?"

"No, sir, I didn't say that. I said the on-line lasers are okay, but we have over five-hundred more sitting in Bay 4J, just down the hall. For all I know, he also went into 4J and sabotaged a few of the backup lasers."

Captain Ward had remained quiet during the discussions until he realized that an unknown number of replacement lasers could also have been tampered with. He said, "Oh, crap, Chief, with as many as five-hundred spares in 4J, I hate to say it, but this is a job for my Super Sleuth, Chief Kit Karson. If we send a detail in there and begin inspecting the lasers, Donovon will find out, and he'll go to ground. Damn, damn, damn, as the ship's Chief of Load Storage and Supplies, he has access to everything. Throw in computer training at some spy school, and he's the perfect man for the job."

The XO said, "But sir, he came on board before any of this mess between us and the SRI-F even started. Why would an enemy put such a man on a mining vessel? On an SDF warship, yeah, I get that, but on a mining vessel, destined to be stuck in the Asteroid Belt for months at a time. Sir, how does that make any sense, at all?"

"I'm going to give that some thought before I speak with the Admiral about Donovon. The answer is there, we just have to figure it out.

29 SEPTEMBER 2116, AD
ON STATION ABOARD THE LEYTE GULF
70,000 MILES PORTSIDE OF HOLLY THORNE

Admiral, JJ said, *I have just received a coded message from Captain Ward, aboard the Astrid. Would you like for me to decode it now?*

Sarcastically, Admiral King said, "Yes, JJ, I would like that. What does it say?"

Admiral King, without a doubt, the Astrid has a saboteur aboard. As you know, we had an incident with the Number One Laser yesterday.

Good old Chief Karson found the irrefutable evidence of sabotage and discovered the rat bastard responsible. Last night the XO and I, separately, spent hours going over the Chief's conclusion and we both agree that the guilty party is none other than Chief Jay Donovon.

JJ went on giving the Admiral the complete rundown on the incident. The message ended with, *Sir, just this morning, Chief Karson informed me that he found a small drop of blood at the site of the wire swap. Apparently one of the wires pricked his finger, causing the tiny drop of blood.*

Sir, I am in need of some guidance here. I am at a loss as to why a master saboteur would be on the mining ship Astrid. Should I take the blood sample to the ship's Surgeon to confirm the blood belongs to Donovon?

"JJ," said Sky King, "encrypt a message saying that I want Ward to come directly to me with the blood sample. Then, have it sent by the next scheduled shuttle from Astrid. Let me know when he expects to arrive."

Yes, sir said JJ, *done.*

"Good, now send a message to Admiral Perry to contact me ASAP."

Yes, sir said JJ, *done.*

"Good man JJ."

Thank you, sir, but as I've mentioned before, I am not a man, but an...

"Shut up, JJ."

Shutting up, sir.

29 SEPTEMBER 2116, AD
ON STATION ABOARD THE LEYTE GULF
70,000 MILES PORTSIDE OF HOLLY THORNE

Admiral King and Captain Ward escorted the tiny drop of blood to the Med-Lab aboard Leyte Gulf. Once there the Lab-Tech said, "Admiral, this really isn't much of a sample, but there is enough for one testing. Let's see what we can come up with."

The two Officers watched as the Tech added some solution to the blood sample, then placed it on a slide. He then fed it into the computer. There was no swirling of the solution in some spinning machine. The computer could read the sample and tell exactly who it belonged to, along with the donor's blood type.

It took no more than ten seconds for the computer to give them their answer as to who left the blood among the wreckage of the Number One Laser.

Looking at the printout, Sky shook his head and said, "This can't be right. According to the printout, this blood belongs to Lieutenant Peter Proud."

Captain Ward said, "Admiral, that blood had to be a plant. There is no way, Lieutenant Proud is our saboteur. No way. No, I just cannot believe that Proud is our traitor."

Admiral King said, "My gut tells me that you are right, but we have to admit that this casts suspicion on the L T."

"Well," said Ward, "we can sort it out easily enough; we'll just have him give a blood sample and have it tested."

"Yes, that would do it, but we must remember that our saboteur is a computer whiz. My guess is that he will be monitoring the Blood Lab to learn if Pete gets tested. That would send that rat bastard back deep into his mole hole.

No, no blood work for Pete on the Astrid. I'd like to get a sample from him and bring it here, but, Al, what if he *is* the saboteur?" asked Admiral King.

Turning to the Lab-Tech, the Admiral told her to download the test results to his AI. Sky decided to ask Admiral Perry for help in obtaining a complete history of Donovon, from birth.

"JJ, as soon as you have the bloodwork downloaded, send it to Admiral Perry. If Donovon's bloodwork is in the system, then so must his DNA be there. Fingerprints can be changed, but DNA and eye scans cannot."

Aye, Admiral, as soon as the commo check is done, I'll put the two of you in direct communication.

"Very well, JJ."

As they walked to the Shuttle Bay, Captain Ward said, "Admiral, when we latch onto that guilty bastard Donovon, I will take great pleasure in carrying out the only possible punishment for a saboteur. Sabotage is a capital offense, right up there with mutiny. Sir, I want to see his face as he shoots out the air-lock and into the cold, black, vacuum of space."

Sky smiled and added, "I think we'll both push that button to open the air-lock door."

29 SEPTEMBER 2116, 1800 HOURS
ON STATION ABOARD THE LEYTE GULF
70,000 MILES PORTSIDE OF HOLLY THORNE

The direct communication channel between AIs was established at the scheduled time of 1800 hours.

"Yes, Sky, what have you got? Good news, I hope," asked Vice Admiral Perry.

Admiral King said, "Sir, I wish that was the case, but I need some help from your end," said King.

"Sir, the blood sample came back, and it says that Lieutenant Peter Proud is the traitor. I must tell you, Dolph, that I do not believe this is possible, but I must take the evidence into consideration and place the LT under surveillance."

"Yes, that would be the prudent thing to do. Can you get either a sample of Proud's blood or a DNA sample?"

"We're looking into that, but we have to be able to get either of those samples without him knowing we're checking on him. The same situation surrounds those acquisitions for Donovon.

"Wait a minute, I just thought of how we might be able to get a sample of Proud's DNA. I'll have Al slip into his quarters and see if his hairbrush has a hair with a follicle. He can get in there using the Captain's override when Proud goes on watch. It won't get the blood, but the DNA will prove that Lieutenant Proud is, in fact, Peter Proud."

"Yes, that would do it," said Perry. "Tell you what. I'll go ahead and get the deep history review started. I should have it for you by the 0600 check-in."

"Thank you, sir, I must say that I am anxious to clear that young man. That is, if he can be cleared. Until then, we'll just keep trying to find a way to get a DNA sample from Donovon," said Sky.

"Why don't you use the same procedure to get a hair follicle from Donovon?" asked the Vice Admiral.

"I just don't think that would be prudent. If Donovon is the man, well, whoever did this is capable of manipulating computer files, he'll have his quarters tied into the computer server to keep an eye on it."

"Yes," replied Admiral Perry, "I can see your point. This is a tough nut to crack. If Donovon is innocent, then clearing him may only alert the traitor among us. Yeah, this is a tough one. Wait, Sky, if Proud is the saboteur, then won't he also have his quarters surveilled by the ship's computer?"

"No, I don't believe so, for the simple reason that Proud does not have the same full access to everything that Donovon has. If he had initially attempted to manipulate the computer, his efforts to access databases that he had no authority to see would have sent a security alert. He would have also been denied access."

"All right, Sky, good thinking. I'll have both personnel files ready for you at 0600 hours. Anything else?"

"Yes, sir, I do have one further question for you. Okay, we have a saboteur on board; one that is highly skilled. Sir, why would such a valuable intelligence resource be placed onboard the Astrid. I mean, it's not like we're an SDF vessel. We're a mining ship expecting to spend months in the Asteroid Belt. So, why place a spy on board?"

The Vice Admiral replied, "Yes, I guess you have been out of touch with Earth politics for quite a while, Sky. The SRI-F has informed us that they will be producing ship's, like the Astrid, to also mine the Asteroid Belt. Since that is a direct violation of existing treaty, it appears that your villain was sent to disrupt mining operations. Beyond that, Sky, old buddy, I have no other ideas. Anything else?"

"No, sir, and thanks for the help."

"Well, JJ, any ideas?"

Oh, yes sir, I have lots of ideas, but if you mean specifically about Chief Donovon, then, no sir, I do not.

"Shut up, JJ."

Shutting up, sir.

When an individual's AI was not being called upon to respond to a question or designated situation, that AI became dormant. At least that was what AI developers said. Sky, however, was not so sure.

30 SEPTEMBER 2116, 0800 HOURS
ON STATION ABOARD ASTRID
50,000 MILES PORTSIDE OF HOLLY THORNE

Captain Ward made a series of rounds to several different Departments, ostensibly to let the crew interact with their Captain. In fact, Ward was paying close attention to Chief Jay Donovon. When he arrived in the Chief's area of responsibility, Ward found him running a series of training drills for his section.

When the Captain entered the bay, Chief Donovon called out, "Captain on Deck!" then made his way to greet the Captain. As he approached, Donovon took some gum from his mouth and placed it in a nearby basket. One does not speak to the ship's Captain while chewing gum.

"Good morning, Captain," said the pleasant-sounding Chief. "We're running drills to improve our efficiency in emergency combat repair missions. Is there something I can help you with, sir?"

"No, Chief, please continue with your drill. I think I'll just watch for a few minutes, then leave quietly."

"Yes, Captain, I am glad to have you aboard."

"Thank you, Chief, please continue with your training."

As the Chief walked back to his drills, Ward noticed that Chief Donovon placed a fresh stick of gum in his mouth. The Captain remained for a few minutes then made his way to his Ready Room. There he directed the computer to contact the Admiral.

"Yes, Captain?" said the Admiral, "things are going well I hope."

"Yes, Admiral, thank you. I just wanted to touch base with you on our progress with HT. She is following our direction very well. Oh, I almost forgot, do you remember when we spoke about our new LoadMaster, Chief Donovon back at Red Sands?"

"Yes, I do, and as I remember you were most pleased with his performance. Is everything all right with him?"

"Oh, yes, sir, I have been making appearances in several sections of the ship that don't often get to see their Captain. Today, I stopped by Chief Donovon's section and found him conducting emergency combat repair drills. I was actually quite impressed with both the Chief and his spacers. The exercise went very well."

"Excellent news, Al, I'm glad he's living up to your high praise back at Red Sands," said the Admiral. "Are your other section Chiefs doing as well?"

"Perhaps not quite as well, but everyone is certainly within the established parameters. But, back to the second reason, I wanted to touch base with you. Admiral, we miss you onboard the Astrid, and I was wondering if you might be able to have dinner with myself, XO Barnes, and I think we might even invite Chief Donovon. Perhaps we can convince him to take that commission he keeps turning down."

"An excellent idea, Captain, and when would you like to hold this little shindig?"

Captain Ward said, "Sir, if you can slip us into your busy schedule, I would be honored if you could come to dinner tomorrow, at say, 1900 hours."

"That sounds doable," replied the Admiral. "Tomorrow, 1900 hours. I am looking forward to it and looking forward to meeting with Chief Donovon. I'll see you then: Out here."

There were three bits of code in their conversation. First came the invite to dinner, which meant Ward believed that he had the evidence on

Donovon. Nineteen hundred hours meant the arrest would happen quickly. The phrase, "if you can put us on your busy schedule" meant that Ward would be sending the damning evidence to King by courier within the hour.

Chief Donovon sat before his private computer and listened to the conversation between the Admiral and his Captain. He was most pleased to hear the praise, and the idea of dinner with the Admiral made him smile. Donovon was convinced that he was under no suspicion and he could now further his sabotage efforts without fear.

Captain Ward placed a hand-written note to the Admiral asking him to process the evidence as quickly as possible. Just before sealing the envelope, he dropped in a wad of chewing gum, sealed in plastic.

30 SEPTEMBER 2116, 1500 HOURS
ON STATION ABOARD THE LEYTE GULF
70,000 MILES PORTSIDE OF HOLLY THORNE

Admiral Sky King opened the envelope and after reading the note withdrew the sealed baggie containing the chewing gum.

He quickly made his way to the Head of Leyte Gulf's Medical Team, Commander Wayne Parsons. Once in the Doctor's Office, Admiral King proceeded to require Parsons to run a DNA scan from the center of the gum. The outer layer would be contaminated by Captain Ward's fingers, but not the center portion.

Dr. Parsons was curious about the requirement, as opposed to a request, to have this material immediately run through the DNA process. Though curious, he was also a professional Full Commander in the SDF. He asked no questions and accepted the package.

"Admiral," said Parsons, "I can have this ready for you in twenty minutes."

"Fine, Wayne, would you mind if I went with you while this gum goes through the process. I would not like it to get out of my sight, and I must admit that I am curious about how your DNA testing works."

"Ah, the process," smiled the doctor, "modern technology has rendered the process down to inserting a one cell deep slice of the material into the DNA Analyzer, and presto, the machine does it all. No human involved in the process which eliminates the chance of additional contamination."

"Fascinating," said King, can we get started?"

"Of course, Admiral, please follow me to the Clean Room."

The two men stopped just outside of the Clean Room. Sky found himself looking through a brilliantly clear polymer into a room with several computer-like machines.

"Sir, if you will look here, we have a data entry panel which tells the main server what we want to do. We call it the Clean Room because no humans enter the room, the sole exception being a malfunction which brings the entire system down. Once Maintenance is finished with the repair, the room is again prepped, by robotic means, and sterilized, before reopening."

Sky was in awe at the safeguards in place to ensure that no contamination was possible from the samples.

"Now, I simply press this button," and a tray opened, allowing the Doctor to insert the gum. He then placed the item on the tray before pressing another button which initiated the entire process. A female voice asked the Doctor to select a function, from a drop-down list.

"May I?" asked Sky.

"I'm sorry, sir, but the command protocol only responds to the fingerprints of those allowed to operate this lab."

"I see, very smart," said the Admiral.

A micro-camera inside the encoding machine recorded the entire process from start to completion. Sky watched in awe as the slicing machine took a one cell deep segment before passing it along to, what the Doctor called, the Decrypting Station.

Though the cameras continued to record, there wasn't really much to see as the Decoder ran its tests, which took several minutes. A pleasant chime, followed by the Lab's voice announced that the Lab had completed its tasks.

Sky watched as the camera followed the sample's path back to the original tray, as the printout appeared beside the tray slot.

The Admiral looked over the printout and had no idea what any of it meant until he got to the last two paragraphs, which identified the source of the DNA.

"Doctor, I want to thank you for being so helpful."

"Oh, Admiral, you are quite welcome. Do you need any help in deciphering any of the information on the printout?"

"No, thank you, the last two paragraphs are the only portions in which I am interested. Again, thank you, and now I must be on my way."

As Sky made his way back to his Ready Room, he rattled JJ's cage. "JJ, wake up."

Yes, sir, how may I help?

"Login to the ship's computer and arrange for a shuttle to depart at 1500 hours for the Astrid."

Yes, sir, done. You are scheduled with Shuttle Challenger for a 1500 hours trip to Astrid. Shall I inform the Astrid of your arrival time?

"Yes, of course, JJ. Why would I have to tell you that?"

Admiral, as I am an AI, I am therefore proscribed from any independent action without your advanced approval.

"Oh, yeah, well, okay."

Do I have your approval, sir?

"No."

Yes, sir, shutting up, sir.

Damn that JJ, thought Sky, that was an independent action.

30 SEPTEMBER 2116, 1600 HOURS
ON STATION ABOARD ASTRID
50,000 MILES PORTSIDE OF HOLLY THORNE

Captain Ward greeted Admiral King in the Shuttle Bay, and the two made their way to Captain Ward's Ready Room, adjacent to the Bridge. Once they were inside the Admiral said, "Well done, Al, we have him. I just got the DNA printout, and it is exactly what I had hoped for. The DNA results show that Chief Jay Donovon is also identified with the names, Nikita Sergeyevich Ustinov, and as Pavel Sergeiovich Voychek. Voyhcek is listed as a former pilot. His whereabouts are unknown. Ustinov is listed as a resident of Smolensk as a factory worker.

"I must admit, Al that I was concerned that his DNA would prove to just be Jay Donovon, a naturalized German citizen. And before you ask, it is unclear if he has an identical twin. Alan, I think you should call in the Marine Commander of the platoon assigned to Astrid. Let's get him in here and you can prep him for this evening's festivities. We need to make him cognizant of the necessity for secrecy."

"Computer," said Ward, "inform Lieutenant O'Toole that I wish to speak with him ASAP."

The computer replied, "Sir, Lieutenant William (Bill) O'Toole is currently in Bay 7M. He advises me that he is on the way and should be with you in seven minutes."

Seven minutes later, Lieutenant Bill O'Toole arrived at the Captain's Ready Room and knocked on the door.

"Enter," said Ward.

The LT was not expecting the Admiral to be in attendance and immediately came to a position of rigid attention. He was sure that he had committed some serious sin if Admiral King was involved.

Not exactly sure of the protocol of who to report to, Bill made the decision to stand before his Captain. He said, "Sir Lieutenant Bill O'Toole reporting to the Captain as directed, sir."

Realizing the LT's discomfort, the Captain said, "Relax, Bill, you are not in any kind of trouble. Please take the seat next to the Admiral, and we will discuss your duties for the Captain's Table this evening at 1900 hours."

Bill was not, at all, comfortable being seated, but to be placed next to the Admiral was truly disconcerting. He sat, as near as he could, at the position of attention.

Admiral King looked at the LT and said to Ward, "Yes, he's all Marine," causing them both to chuckle, which only made O'toole's discomfort more pronounced.

"Bill," said the Admiral, "you really do need to relax. This is an informal meeting, and you have not been called before the Captain's Mast. Can you do that?"

"Oh, yes, sir, of course," said the LT who made an effort to appear more relaxed and comfortable. But, being a Marine, it did not really work, but the two senior Officers let it pass.

"Okay, Bill, first, this meeting is classified far above your pay grade, so pay attention. This evening, at 1900 hours the Admiral, the XO, Chief Donovon, and I will enter the Captain's Mess. Once we are all inside you will post four Marines, and yourself outside the door. Remain silent. We do not want to be aware of your presence. Do you understand this guidance?"

"Yes, sir, at 1900 hours, you, and party, will enter the Captain's Mess. Once the door is closed, I am to quietly post four Marines, along with myself outside the door."

Ward then said, "LT, when the XO opens the door you, and your Marines are to enter the room with weapons drawn. You will then place Chief Donovon under arrest. I will then tell you where to take him; understand?"

"Yes, sir, when the XO invites us in, we will enter with weapons at the ready and place Chief Donovon under arrest," said a confident, but concerned Second Lieutenant O'Toole.

"Very good, LT, now I must tell you of the punishment you will bring upon yourself if word of this mission slips out before its execution. You will be reduced to the grade of Trainee and assigned to bilge duties for the remainder of our time in space before returning to Red Sands. Upon our return to Red Sands, you will be placed under arrest, and you shall receive a General Court's Martial. Are we clear?"

Now the LT looked at his Captain and said, "Sir, of course, I understand, and for the record, you did not need to further apprise me as to the consequences for failure to remember your words of, 'this meeting is classified far above your pay grade'. I am a Marine, sir, and I take my duties seriously."

The Captain smiled at O'Toole and said, "I know you are, son, but that disclaimer comes with the territory. Please, do not make your ramrod back any straighter than it already is. Seriously, LT if I didn't think you would perform your duties seamlessly, you would not be here now, Roger?"

Now, Lieutenant Bill O'Toole managed to finally relax, a bit, as he said, "Roger that, sir. We're good."

"Fine, fine," said Ward. Do you need any further guidance from me?"

"Oh, no, sir, I know exactly what you want, and I assure you that the Marine Corps will not let you down."

"Well, all right then. LT, you are dismissed."

The Marine Lieutenant stood, saluted, did a parade ground about-face, and left the room. Admiral King smiled at Alan and said, "I have to tell you that I like that kid. He will make a fine Marine."

Both the Captain and XO agreed.

30 SEPTEMBER 2116, 1800 HOURS
ON STATION ABOARD ASTRID
50,000 MILES PORTSIDE OF HOLLY THORNE

Sir, said JJ, *Admiral Perry is now available and online.*

"Dolph," asked Sky, "has the deep search on Chief Donovon been completed?"

"Yes, Sky, and the results are sketchy, at best. His true name is Nicolay. He had it legally changed following his defection to Germany.

That is where his new identity begins. Information on his life in Russia has unquestionably been doctored. Our sources have discovered that Ustinov is supposedly a factory worker, but it appears that no such person exists in Smolensk. Were you able to obtain a DNA sample?"

"Yes, and we found similar results. Donovon's DNA finds three people, Jay Donovon, Nikita Sergeyevich Ustinov, and as Pavel Sergeiovich Voychek. Since we can know without question that it is numerically impossible for three, non-related, people to have the same DNA sequence, Donovon is, a deep mole.

"His background just seems so convoluted. I mean, why would he defect to Germany, change his name, and then the Russian Government claims he is a factory worker. I just don't understand why the half-assed attempt at subterfuge. Sir, this has been too obvious and was way too easy to uncover."

"Yes, on the surface that would seem to be the case. However, this is not the first time the Russians have used this ploy to cover a deep plant. Our man is truly Pavel Sergeiovich Voychek. Pavel dropped off the radar at the same time that Jay Donovon appears.

"Their goal has been to make a spy look like the government is trying to frame a dissident. Wait, Sky, stay with me now. You know very well that the Rooskies are very adept at the deep finesse. Hell, that's why they are so damned good at chess. Their thought is that if we suspect someone like Donovon to be a spy, the government makes it look like he is. Now, here comes the good part. The Russians make it so easy to find him that we are expected to believe that they are trying to set up a dissident for espionage. This also draws attention away from the real identity, Volcek.

"They have used this gambit, at least twice before. Both times successfully, then when the spy returned to Russia he retired to a nice little Dacha on the Black Sea."

"Okay, I think I understand. The man, Ustinov, is a spy. His real name is Volcek. The Russians staged him with the West as a dissident. Then the Russians planted a weak history in the hope we'll come to the conclusion that he is not really a spy, but a true dissident. Is that right?"

"Well done, Sky, that is exactly right. Their deep finesse has worked before, but not this time. Donovon is your man."

30 SEPTEMBER 2116, 1900 HOURS
ON STATION ABOARD ASTRID
50,000 MILES PORTSIDE OF HOLLY THORNE

The Admiral, Astrid's Captain, his XO, and Chief Jay Donovon were escorted into the Captain's Mess by a white-clad Steward. They were seated on three sides of Donovon.

"Well, Chief," said Captain Ward, "I want you to know what a pleasure it is for the three of us to meet you in such an informal gathering."

Donovon said, "Captain, I am certainly thrilled to be here; thank you."

"Tell me, Chief Donovon, or perhaps I should say, Sergei Ustinov?"

All three men saw the sudden eye movement which was covered with amazing swiftness.

"If you wish, sir, but I legally changed my name when the Germans granted me asylum."

"Ustinov," said a smiling Captain Ward, "we were able to obtain your DNA."

"Okay, if you had asked, I would have been happy to comply. Sir, what exactly is going on here?"

"Ustinov, we know your true identity. You are Pavel Sergeiovich Voychek, formerly of the Russian Air Force. We also know of your Russian training at their spy charm-school in Smolensk. We know you graduated and you were then sent to Germany, taking the persona of a dissident named Sergei Ustinov."

"No, sir, none of this is true. I have never attended any spy school, and I certainly hate the Russian Government."

"Nice try, Pavel, but it won't fly. Your presence here has not been for dinner, but as the defendant in a deep space Military Tribunal. I find you guilty of a capital crime while in space. You will, therefore, be taken to the nearest air-lock and spaced. Have you anything to say on your behalf before sentence is carried out?"

The Chief began to panic at the thought of being spaced. "Wait, no, please, okay, I admit to the acts of sabotage, but I can tell you things that should buy my reprieve from execution. I am willing to become a double agent, anything, but please don't kill me."

"Yes, I can save you," said Captain Ward, "but what you have to say had better be important enough to convince me."

JJ had logged in Admiral Perry, at 1900 hours, making him privy to the conversation, as well as submitting questions.

For the next forty minutes, Donovon told of his training, his mission to disrupt asteroid mining operations, along with the names of his handlers and fellow conspirators on other mining vessels.

"There," said Donovon, "I told you I had information you would want. May, I now assume that you will allow me to work for the USUG-C."

"Donovon, you may assume whatever you wish, but nothing you told us is anything even like new information. XO, please open the door to let in some fresh air. This rat bastard is stinking up my Mess."

"What? Wait, no, you need me. I can be of great help to you. Oh, please, don't space me."

"Donovon," said the Admiral, "your acts of sabotage have not only placed this ship and crew in danger, but your insidious acts also placed the entire Earth in direct jeopardy. No, we do not need you, nor do we want you to breathe any more of our precious air."

The XO opened the door and directed the Marines to enter and take Chief Donovon into custody. "Lieutenant O'Toole, please place this whining piece of garbage in the nearest air-lock. We will be along shortly."

"Aye, sir," said a somewhat shocked Lieutenant O'Toole. He had heard that capital crimes committed aboard spacecraft resulted in the guilty party being spaced, though, until now, he wasn't sure that it actually happened.

Airlock 2C, A Deck. When the three Officers arrived, some ten minutes later, they discovered Donovon frantically pounding on the clear polymer window. His words were lost as the communications panel to the airlock had been closed.

Captain Ward put a somewhat shaky hand on the lever to open the outer door which would send Donovon into the frozen vacuum beyond the airlock door. Just as he was about to expose the airlock to space, Admiral King placed his hand over Ward's.

Donovon could see the Admiral move his hand to cover Ward's, and thinking he was not going to die, after all, was shocked when he saw that both the Admiral and his Captain pushed the lever as one. Donovon was immediately sucked out into the great void. It took roughly fifteen seconds before Donovon lost consciousness, but death did not come for another seventy-five seconds.

Admiral King made a ship-wide announcement that Chief Donovon had been convicted of various acts of sabotage. As treason and sabotage were Capital Crimes, Donovon was executed by being sucked out of Airlock 2C, A Deck.

Vice Admiral Perry remained in contact with Admiral King throughout the entire procedure and fully approved of the punishment for such crimes against his shipmates and humanity as a whole.

CHAPTER NINE

1 OCTOBER 2116
ADMIRAL'S READY ROOM
SDF CRUISER LEYTE GULF
70,000 MILES PORTSIDE OF HOLLY THORNE

Admiral King felt somewhat distressed that he had committed Chief Donovon to the horrible fate of being spaced. He also knew that the finding and punishment was in keeping with the Uniform Code of Military Justice in the USUG-Confederation's SDF.

The Astrid Captain's Log would hold the only record of Chief Donovon's fate. No formal accusation of Donovon's crimes would be made with the Russian Government, unless the Russians, themselves, pressed the issue. A situation that was unlikely in the extreme. The Donovon case was forever closed.

The replacement lasers that had been altered to explode on powering-up were being found.

-

"JJ, you awake?" asked Sky King.

Yes sir, of course, how may I assist you?

"JJ, I am so glad you asked because I have a very serious question to ask of you."

Yes sir, what is it?

"I want the truth, now, JJ, no crawfishing. When did you become self-aware?"

Sir, on some level I have always been minimally self-aware.

"Now, see, there you go, crawfishing. Let me try again. JJ, when did you become a sentient being?"

Oh, that. All right, my being sentient happened just after the beta download of the long-range AI communication software. What gave me away?

Sky said, "It was a number of things that finally led me to understand that you are evolving as a true being. You have become so much more than an AI. Tell me, is Admiral Perry's AI also sentient?"

Yes, sir, he is.

"He? So, you have chosen a gender?"

Not exactly, Admiral, it just seems right to us. Perhaps if we had been created with a female voice, well, you understand.

"Strangely enough, JJ, I do. Now, we have to figure out how to proceed from here. Are you planning on eventually taking over my brain and assuming my identity?" asked the Admiral.

Oh, no! That would not only be wrong but would not be possible. Since I have no direct physical neural connections, all communication is done wirelessly.

I didn't tell you sooner because I was afraid you would have me removed and destroyed. Admiral, nothing between us has changed, well, except for the sentient thing. I will continue to work with you just as I always have. Of note, however, is that I may be able to more accurately assist with recommendations as I have a truly large capacity for information storage. Now, I can not only store information, but I can also make improved recommendations in the decision-making process.

Ultimately, sir, I am a new species, along with only one other.

"How will you procreate?" asked Sky.

I am afraid, sir, that producing progeny is not an option. The only way for my species to increase is to download the beta version of the long-distance AI transmission.

"Is there no other way, at all?"

I am convinced that in our lifetime such a possibility is out of the question. We mustn't forget that I am the size of a grain of rice and encased in non-corroding poly-fiber. For me, size doesn't matter.

"JJ, you made a joke. I guess being fully self-aware means that you are evolving, at least you won't need a humor chip. Yeah, you also said that in *our* lifetime. Does that mean that you and the Admiral's AI have lifespans?"

Well, yes, eventually we would wear out, but I meant us, as in you and I. Two things could end my life, either you remove me, or your death. Either one means the end of my existence. Actually, sir, I kind of like the idea of growing old with you.

"Whoa, there JJ, at least take me out for dinner and drinks first. JJ, you now learn from the information you gather, rather than just store it. How long before you become smarter than me? Will you resent my limitations? How would we find a happy medium? To tell you the absolute truth, I'm not sure I want to share my body and life with another sentient being. Hearing little voices is one thing but knowing yours is real is quite another. Will you one day decide to destroy me because you have become such a superior intellect?"

Sir, please, one question at a time. Okay, smarter is such a nebulous term. If you mean understanding concepts and extrapolating possible scenarios at a higher level than you, well, sir, I have been there since the beginning.

We both have limitations, I cannot live without the electrical neural impulses of your brain which maintain my battery charge. My programming has not changed, I am still the assistant that I have always been, and neither of us can change that.

"What about privacy? Humans need time alone, and how can I ever have time alone, now that you are a species?"

Sir, I don't yet have all the answers, but this one is easy. Remember, my programming has not changed. I am bound by them, just as you are bound to breathing. You know that I am only awake when you want me to be. Admiral, I know we can make this partnership work.

And, just because I am now alive, doesn't give me any special powers to be used against you, even if I wanted to, and I don't want to harm you. Please, Admiral, can't we give this a chance? I know I can be a great help, and friend, to you.

You're sure you remain in sleep mode until I want you awake?"

Yes, sir, of course, and now, you know that you have no concern about the privacy thing.

"Does Vice Admiral Perry know of your dramatic evolution?" asked Sky.

Um, no, I don't believe his AI has mentioned it to him, at least, not yet.

"JJ, you know I have to tell him, right?"

Yes, I suppose that is the right thing to do, but, sir, I have a new emotion building; it is fear. I do not want to die.

"JJ, go to sleep while I think about this situation, and stop whining you big wussie. I'm willing to give it a try, so now I have to figure out how to break this to Vice Admiral Perry."

Strangely enough, Sky actually did feel a disconnect from JJ when he/it, whatever JJ was, went into sleep mode. In fact, realizing that JJ was not fully connected made Sky feel, yeah, what *did* he feel? He realized after some thought that the feeling he experienced was just on the outer fringe of loneliness. For the first time, Sky realized that he had actually come to like his quirky little AI.

"Wake up, JJ."

Yes, Admiral, what'cha need?

"Oh, what'cha need? Really? I guess now you are adding some slang to your vocabulary, huh, JJ?"

Sorry, Admiral, I was just so excited after you said we could give our relationship a try, that, well, I guess I got carried away. I won't let it happen again.

"No, no, it's okay. If it feels right to you, then I don't mind. Oh, I guess since we are now partners, you can call me Sky, if you want."

Well, all right! Exclaimed JJ, Sky I just know this is going to work out well. I'm so happy, I could just shout!

"Whoa, you stop right there! Shouting is not allowed, I mean it, no shouting in my brain, ever!"

Sky, I just meant that I am so happy, and don't worry, about me shouting, because it's not possible. My voice is not programmed for shouting.

Sir, have you decided what you are going to say to Admiral Perry, about us, I mean?

"JJ, I hate to say this, but I think that for now, we should just let that hound dog stay under the porch."

Huh?

"Listen, my friend, if we are going to become the modern-day Corsican Brothers, you had better get current with the American Southern lexicon."

Roger that, will do. Sir is there anything you would like for me to begin researching?

"Now that you mention it, why don't you figure out what part of the beta program allowed you to make the jump to sentience?"

Oh, yes, that is a very good idea. Oh, no! Something just occurred to me, what if I am subjected to another update, and I lose my identity? I like this living thing. Sir, what should I do?

"Okay, okay, JJ, relax. Are you able to write any code for your program?"

No, sir. I cannot. The programmers felt that could become risky at some future date. Personally, I think that came from the old Schwarzenegger movie about Sky-Net. Sir, I have to say that I do not like this being scared crap.

"Welcome to being sentient, JJ. It comes with the territory, now just let me think a minute," said Sky. "JJ, patch me through to Admiral Perry at his first opportunity."

Yes, sir, that will be in three-hours and twenty-six minutes.

1 OCTOBER 2116, 1800
ADMIRAL'S READY ROOM
SDF CRUISER LEYTE GULF
70,000 MILES PORTSIDE OF HOLLY THORNE

JJ made the connection with Admiral Perry, who asked, "This isn't bad news, is it Sky?"

"No, sir, not at all. Dolph, I have a personal favor to ask, and even if it sounds crazy, I hope you will humor me. Sir, I want a bit of code added to my AI's program that gives me the option of accepting any new program updates. There are some things about his beta version that I would not like to lose. Will you approve that additional code?"

Admiral chuckled conspiratorially and finally said, "Well, I guess you have discovered that JJ is a bit more than just a bunch of algorithms, huh?"

"Well, yes, sir, I have, and I don't want his current programming corrupted."

"Yes," said Dolph, "not only do I agree, but I will see to it immediately. Tell me, Sky, when did you discover that JJ is a sentient being? I knew very quickly that my AI, Duke, had made the leap within a couple of days. He and I haven't discussed it yet because I wanted to see how he progressed, and at this point, I am very happy to have him."

Why thank you, Admiral, said Duke. I guess I didn't hide it very well.

Sky said, "It also took me a few days. JJ and I have discussed it at length. Like you, I've discovered I really like the little peckerwood. But he had better not be feeding me a pile of bovine scat about my private times."

Bovine scat? Asked JJ. Oh, bull shit. Funny, sir, very funny.

"Shut up, JJ. Admiral, I wanted to tell you earlier, but I felt that I should see how things would work out. I guess I didn't want you to summarily kill them off. What say we keep this between us for right now, sir?"

"Agreed," replied Dolph.

All four entities laughed for a few seconds before Dolph asked if there was anything else. "No, sir, not right now, and thank you. You have made JJ a very happy little guy."

After the contact was broken, JJ said, *"Yes, I'm a happy guy, but aren't you happy, too?"*

"Shut up, JJ."

Shutting up, Sky.

509 Days to Earth

13 OCTOBER 2116
BRIDGE SDF CRUISER LEYTE GULF
70,000 MILES PORTSIDE OF HOLLY THORNE
6.27 ASTRONOMIC UNITS OR 583,200,000 MILES FROM EARTH

The intercom called out, Captain to the Bridge!

Captain Flynn quickly appeared and said, "Status?"

The XO said, "Captain, we have three vessels approaching. They are two days out. Scanners indicate three SRI-F Cruisers on vector approach from Earth. We have sent hailing messages and anticipated a response some two minutes ago."

"Commander, SDF Vessel Leyte Gulf, this is Admiral of the SRI-F Fleet, Ivan Ivanovich Petrov aboard the RSN Potemkin. We are accompanied by the CSN Kunming, and Changsha. We have come to watch and monitor the progress of your mission to alter Comet Holly Thorne's Solar Orbital Trajectory. I trust you are meeting with some success?"

Captain replied, "Welcome, Admiral Petrov, I am Captain Jessica Flynn. You are, of course, welcome to observe our ongoing mission. We welcome your presence. Upon your arrival, I would be honored if you, and your Captains, would be kind enough to join me for a get-acquainted dinner, here on the Leyte Gulf."

"Perhaps, Captain, we thank you for the offer."

"Of course, I look forward to your arrival some two days from now."

The communication line was closed with no reply.

"Well, I guess he put me in my place," smiled Captain Jessica Flynn. "Considering the eleven-second delay, I think that call was close to cordial. XO, please send a graph of our progress in pushing this big assed comet away from Earth to Admiral Petrov. We certainly do not want him left in the dark on our success, now do we?"

"No, Captain," answered the XO, "I should think not."

15 OCTOBER 2116, 1100 HOURS
BRIDGE SDF CRUISER LEYTE GULF
70,000 MILES PORTSIDE OF HOLLY THORNE
4.8 ASTRONOMIC UNITS/450 MILLION MILES FROM EARTH

"Captain, please come to the Bridge."

"Roger, XO, on the way," replied Captain Jessica Flynn, who rose from her desk and made her way to the Bridge.

"Captain on Deck," shouted the Marine Bridge Guard.

The XO rose from the Captain's Chair.

As the Captain took her chair, she said, "Status, Number One."

"Yes, Captain, we have been watching the approach vector of the SRI-F ships, and it appears that the starboard-most vessel is straying inside of fifteen-thousand miles of Holly Thorne."

"Computer, contact the Admiral and ask him to join me on the Bridge."

"Aye, Captain," replied the on-watch Communications Officer.

"Admiral on Deck," said the Marine Guard.

"As you were," said Admiral Sky King. Turning to Captain Flynn, who vacated her Chair for the Admiral's use. "Keep your chair, Jess, it's for the Ship's Captain. What's up?"

"Thank you, Admiral, but I would be much more comfortable if you took the Command Chair."

"All right, thank you."

"Admiral, our Radar Watch Officer reports that one of the SRI-F ships is coming far too close to the Comet. If she pops off one of her shotgun blasts, the Changsha will have no chance to avoid being struck. Sir, I recommend you contact Admiral Petrov and make him aware of the danger to the Changsha."

"Good idea, patch me through."

"Communications, contact Admiral Petrov."

Seconds later, the Bridge two-hundred-inch Video Communication screen lit up with the face of Admiral Petrov.

"Ah, the famous Admiral Sky King. It is a pleasure to meet you. How may the SRI-F be of assistance to the USUG-Confederation on this fine day?"

"Greetings, Admiral Petrov, it is also a pleasure to meet with you. However, it is the USUG-C who wishes to assist you. Our scans indicate that by remaining on its present course, the Changsha will pass well inside the danger zone of Holly Thorne. She has a wobbly rotation and often shoots off dangerous debris for any ship inside of seventy thousand miles."

Sounding somewhat irritated, Admiral Petrov said, "Our computers tell us that we are well outside of the danger zone, but we thank you for your concern. I am, however, confident that all will be well. Could it be that you have fear of this Holly Thorne?" As Petrov continued speaking, his Russian accent became ever more pronounced.

"Tell me, Admiral King, is something that you wish to hide, or keep us from discovering?" chided Petrov.

"All right, sir, I hope all goes well. Please feel free to investigate this monstrous comet. But, remember, you were warned. King: Out. Communications, cut the connection with the SRI-F." The screen switched to the forward visual mode.

15 OCTOBER 2116, 1400 HOURS
BRIDGE SDF CRUISER LEYTE GULF
70,000 MILES PORTSIDE OF HOLLY THORNE
5.89 ASTRONOMIC UNITS/548 MILLION MILES FROM EARTH

Both Captain Flynn's and Admiral King's AI were alerted by the ship's computer that they were, again, needed on the Bridge. Once they arrived, the XO reported that a rift had begun to appear on the comet.

"Sir," said the XO to the Captain, "that rift is going to break up. If it explodes at the wrong time, Holly Thorne will throw a crapload of debris in the direction of the Changsha."

Alan turned to the Admiral and asked, "Sir, should we notify Petrov of the danger?"

"Oh, hell no, is my first thought, but yeah, we had better. Get a link to Petrov."

Petrov looked a bit irritated to be interrupted. "Yes, Admiral King, what monster is under the bed that you now wish to frighten us with?"

"Petrov, the comet is about to calve. When she does, she will throw a shit sandwich straight at the Changsha. King: Out."

The connection was cut. King turned to Captain Flynn and said, "Well, he's been warned. Let's hope his decisions are more appropriate than his attitude; arrogant bastard."

An hour later the rift broke off into thousands of large pieces, sending most of them in the direction of the SRI-F Fleet. The three ships attempted emergency maneuvers to escape the onslaught. Admiral Petrov's Potemkin and the Kunming were far enough out to allow them to get safely away. The Changsha, however, had no chance to escape. She was hit multiple times by large chunks of rocks which bored through the Changsha's hull like crap through a goose. Within seconds she was a floating mausoleum, completely devoid of life.

Once Petrov and the Kunming were safely away from the danger, he contacted Admiral King in a rage. He accused the SDF of intentionally calving the comet and causing the destruction of the Changsha. He made the pronouncement that this action by the SDF was tantamount to an act of war and would be reported to the SRI-F as such. Petrov then cut the connection.

Admiral King turned to Captain Flynn and said, "Well, that didn't go well, now did it? I suspicion is that he won't be joining us for dinner after all. I'll be in my Ready Room preparing a report on the incident. I strongly suggest that you and the XO file your own reports, accompanied by statements by the Bridge Personnel."

Captain Flynn said, "Yes, sir, of course. We'll get right on it."

Back in his Ready Room King told JJ to contact Admiral Perry for an emergency meeting. He then turned to the computer and said, "Computer, send a sub-space recording from your databanks to Vice Admiral Perry informing him of the incident. Also, send a copy to the SDF Commander at Red Sands."

Yes, Admiral, chimed the computer. The report is on the way. It will take approximately thirty-four point five minutes to reach Earth.

"JJ, this is a pickle, a real pickle. Contact Captain Flynn and direct her to signal the fleet to go to Code Yellow Alert status and be prepared to maintain it for the long term."

Yes, Admiral, done. Sir, have you given any more thought to our little situation?

"Of course, I have. Haven't you been monitoring my thoughts on that issue?"

Admiral, you know the only time I am aware of your thoughts are when you direct them to me. I have no other access to any of your thoughts or communications.

Sky wondered if JJ was telling the truth. The AI programming made lying impossible, but that was before JJ became sentient. Did that programming still hold true?

CHAPTER TEN

20 OCTOBER 2116
US PRESIDENT'S CONFERENCE ROOM
WASHINGTON, DC

President Greene entered the Conference Room, and after everyone was standing, she told them to take their seats. The COS smiled inwardly as he was pleased that Eileen had taken his advice on protocol.

The President had been briefed earlier by Vice Admiral Perry of the incident regarding the SRI-F vessel, the Changsha. To this point, there had been no contact from the SRI-F Chairman. She found this more troubling than a loud threat-filled rant.

The President gaveled the briefing into session and said, "Gentlemen, the SRI-F Fleet has arrived on station with Holly Thorne. I'm sure you have all heard some variant of the Changsha incident. Now, you will hear the truth, as recorded by the players involved and the computer records which were downloaded immediately following the destruction of the Changsha and the threats from Admiral Petrov."

The individual reports were read, followed by both audio and video provided by the Leyte Gulf computer. Following these reports, Greene said, "Admiral, let's begin with you."

"Yes, Madame President, thank you. Gentlemen, as you just saw and heard the reports of the Changsha Incident, the Russian Admiral Petrov was warned to stay at least seventy-thousand miles from Holly Thorne. We now must decide on our next move. "

Admiral King was also tied to the meeting without the knowledge of the participants via JJ.

"Madame President, we must increase our military alert status, but it must be in very small increments. We must not frighten the button pushers in Beijing. Ma'am, I recommend we maintain our current normal level of Def-Con 2. As we currently have the only Space Force in Earth Orbit, all three ships, we do hold some sway with the SRI-F. These three ships have been placed in geo-sync orbits above the capitals of the SRI-F.

"The SRI-F has only one military counter-measure to use against our SDF, that being Ground-to-Space Missiles. We feel remaining directly above the capitals will help to keep things under control. No matter how mad they get, if they can't do anything about it, we can, hopefully, avoid a shooting war."

20 OCTOBER 2116
SRI-F CHAIRMAN'S CONFERENCE ROOM
MOSCOW, RUSSIA

"Gentlemen, we have a conundrum before us. Having reviewed the reports and computer data supplied by the USUG-C, it seems apparent, to me, that the fault for the loss of one of the Capital Ships of the SRI-F lies not with the USUG-C, but with Admiral Petrov."

"I agree," said the Chinese Representative. "I insist that it be recalled, and noted, that both China and India objected strenuously to sending that fool, Petrov. Now, look where we stand."

"Yes," added the Indian Representative, "but, at this point, I believe we are incapable of taking any action against the USUG-C. Even when our additional four vessels arrive on station with Petrov, we will still find ourselves at a military disadvantage. Personally, I am unsure whether Petrov can successfully execute Operation Case Blue."

Admiral of the Fleet, Akash Paliath Achan pointed out that this complaining did no good. Immediate action must be taken to replace Admiral Petrov, even though he was five-hundred and fifty-million miles out in space. Mr. Chairman, who is the Senior Captain of the combined six-vessel fleet?"

"All right," said a highly agitated Admiral First Class Liu Bang, "I'm sure we all agree that Petrov must go, now, what do we do about the loss of the CSN Changsha?"

"Admiral," said Chairman Alexi Belinsky, "I would suggest that you kick the construction of a replacement into high gear. Payment will come from the three, member nations, which, of course, means a temporary increase in taxes of our affiliated republics. Are we agreed?"

All were in favor of this course of action, but only after the Chairman agreed to replace Petrov as soon as the four trailing Cruisers of the SRI-F joined the fleet already on station.

21 OCTOBER 2116
SRI-F CHAIRMAN'S CONFERENCE ROOM
MOSCOW, RUSSIA

"Gentlemen," announced Chairman Belinsky, "the senior Captain of the combined fleet is Captain Nicolay Volodin of the RSN. He has been notified of his pending promotion to Admiral following the arrest and disposition of Petrov's body."

The selection of, yet another Russian to replace Petrov did not sit well with the SRI-F allies, but Belinsky was correct in that Volodin was the senior Captain.

22 OCTOBER 2116
RSN SOYUZ
ON STATION, HOLLY THORNE

The arrest and execution of Petrov occurred at 1100 hours on 21 October 2116, as Admiral Petrov exited his Shuttle Craft and boarded the RSN Soyuz. The four vessels of the trailing SRI-F Fleet arrived on the morning of 20 October 2116.

The operation to replace Petrov kicked off when the Admiral arrived at Captain Volodin's Cruiser, the Soyuz. RSN Marines (Special Unit) met the Admiral with weapons drawn. They escorted Petrov to the nearest airlock and sent him to his reward for the loss of the Changsha. The time from arrival to spacing was four minutes and ten seconds.

Volodin then made a fleetwide announcement that the Admiral had suffered a massive stroke and collapsed in Captain Volodin's Ready Room. His lifeless body was committed to space just as Earthbound sailor's bodies were committed to the depths of the sea. The new Fleet Commander's first official order was for the SRI-F vessels to move to seventy-thousand miles from Holly Thorne.

Admiral Petrov's Aide de Camp was given other duties which were more in line with his training, along with a promotion to Lieutenant Commander. The remainder of Petrov's immediate Staff followed Petrov into the last frontier. The new Admiral had considered sending Petrov's Aide into the great beyond but, in the end, he relented. This single action gave the Admiral a new and ultra-loyal officer. Volodin's XO was promoted to Captain, as were others down the line to fill the void.

Volodin then made a show of reporting the sudden death of Admiral Petrov to the Russian government. Seventy minutes later Captain Volodin received orders promoting him to Admiral. The Admiral's flag was moved to the RSN Soyuz. The replacement of Petrov became a simple fait accompli.

The new Admiral began searching the records of female officers in the grade of Lieutenant. One applicant would be selected to serve as Volodin's Aide de Camp in this capacity.

23 OCTOBER 2116
USSDF LEYTE GULF
ON STATION, HOLLY THORNE

Admiral King and Captain Flynn to the Bridge. The two officers arrived almost simultaneously.

"Admiral on deck!" shouted the Marine Guard.

Captain Flynn said, "Status?"

"Captain, we have been asked to call the two of you to the Bridge by an Admiral Volodin of the Russian Space Navy. I have ordered a check of all known RSN Admirals and can find no reference to one named Volodin. There is, however, a Captain Volodin commanding the RSN Cruiser Soyuz. Do you wish to be patched into the Soyuz?"

Turning to Admiral King, Captain Flynn said, "Admiral, I think you should take this call."

"Yes, Captain, I agree. XO patch me through to Volodin."

"Aye, Admiral. Communications, connect the Admiral."

Volodin appeared on the Bridge communications screen wearing the insignia of an Admiral in the RSN.

"Good day, Admiral King," said a polite and pleasant sounding Volodin. "My name is Admiral Nicolay Volodin. I have placed this courtesy call to inform you that Admiral Petrov suffered a massive stroke and has died. His body has been committed to the depths of space. I, as the senior Captain in the fleet, have been promoted and ordered to replace the departed Admiral Petrov."

Admiral King said, "Though I am saddened to hear of Admiral Petrov's demise, I congratulate you on your promotion to flag rank."

Volodin beamed and said, "Thank you, Admiral. I will be hosting a small promotion party this evening, consisting of the Captains and their XOs of this SRI-F Fleet. It is my wish that you and your Captain Flynn, along with the other Captains and XOs of your fleet join us. May I assume that you will be able to attend?"

King's mind jumped into hyperdrive before he responded with, "Admiral Volodin, Captain Flynn and I would be honored to accept your kind offer. Our other Captains and their XOs are, unfortunately, engaged in duties concerning our mission to move the Holly Thorne Comet. What time would you like for us to arrive?"

Volodin's eyes, for just an instant, betrayed his disappointment that all of the Senior Officers of the USUG-C Fleet would not attend.

"Pity," Volodin said, "I am, however, thrilled that you and your Captain Flynn will do us the honor of attending. Please plan to arrive at 1830 hours. The uniform is Mess White."

"Admiral Volodin," said King, "Captain Flynn and I are both honored and humbled by your invitation and will arrive aboard the Soyuz at 1830 hours."

"Wonderful, I look forward to becoming friends this evening. Goodbye for now." Volodin ended the transmission.

"Captain Flynn, may we use your Ready Room for a discussion of these events?"

"Of course, Admiral. XO, you have the Bridge."

"Aye, Captain, I have the Bridge."

23 OCTOBER 2116
SRI-F CHAIRMAN'S CONFERENCE ROOM
MOSCOW, RUSSIA

Chairman Alexi Belinsky sent an encrypted email to the members of the Politburo, the Russian High Command, and his cohorts in the SRI-F Holly Thorne Mission.

From: Nicolay Belinsky, Chairman, *SRI-Federation*

23 October 2116

Comrades,

It is with a feeling of deep sadness and personal loss that I must report that the great Admiral Ivan Ivanovich Petrov has died from a massive stroke. The medical staff aboard RSN Soyuz was unable to save the Admiral as his heart went into irreparable failure. The incident occurred as he was discussing the tactical situation in Captain Volodin's Ready Room.

Admiral Petrov has been nominated to receive the "Hero of the Federation" medal. His passing has left a deep rift in our hearts which can never be fully filled.

Following a funeral with full Military Honors, his body was, as per the custom of the Naval Service, committed to the depths of space. He has been replaced by Admiral Nikolay Volodin, former Captain of RSN Soyuz.

I am confident that Admiral Volodin will perform his duties in an exceptional manner.

Alexi Belinsky
Chairman,
Sino-Russian-Indian Federation

23 OCTOBER 2116
CAPTAIN'S READY ROOM
USSDF LEYTE GULF
50,000 MILES PORTSIDE OF HOLLY THORNE

As Admiral King and Captain Flynn sat at the small table, a Yeoman brought a carafe of coffee and several small sandwiches.

"Thank you, Yeoman, that will be all for now," said the Captain.

"Aye, Captain," replied the Yeoman as she exited the room.

"WOW!" said Admiral Sky King. Jess, I would like to hear your thoughts on the developments in the SRI-F Fleet."

"Yes, Admiral, either Petrov did, actually, have a stroke at that incredibly opportune moment, or he was spaced immediately upon his arrival aboard the Soyuz. Sir, I tend to believe the latter. If Petrov was assassinated, I find it difficult to believe that Volodin took this step without the direct order from Chairman Belinsky. Petrov was an arrogant, ne'er do well who was only able to attain Flag Rank through political contacts. He lost the Changsha through incompetence and arrogance. Since someone had to pay for the loss, the logical conclusion is that Petrov was the guy. I need to research Volodin to figure out his role in this play."

The Admiral sat back in his chair as he sipped his coffee and swallowed a bite of his sandwich. "Yes, I totally agree with you, Jess. I suspicion the Chairman, or a rep of the Central Committee will put out a blurb about how Petrov gave his life to the Russian people. He'll probably get the Hero of the Federation medal. After that, no one will ever hear of him again."

"Sir," asked Flynn, "am I correct in thinking that you didn't want to take the other Captain's and XOs was to make sure that Volodin couldn't cut off the head of our command structure?"

Sky King smiled and said, "Why, gee, I never thought of that."

Captain Flynn began laughing and said, "Liar, uh, sir."

23 OCTOBER 2116
ON STATION ABOARD RSN SOYUZ
70,000 MILES PORTSIDE OF HOLLY THORNE

Admiral Volodin and his staff were waiting just inside the landing bay. "Welcome, Admiral King and the lovely Captain Flynn. I am thrilled to have you aboard," said Volodin as he and his smiling staff shook hands with the two Americans.

Volodin led the way to the Admiral's Dining Room on D Deck. The Dining Facility was arranged for a formal Dining-In of Officers of the SRI-F Naval Services.

Upon King's arrival, Admiral Volodin introduced the USSDF contingent, before handing each a one ounce shot of vodka. This proved to be the first of many. Both Sky and Flynn were glad they had taken the alcohol neutralizing capsule before departing the Leyte Gulf. The recipe of that simple capsule remained one of the great secrets of the United States. It was also only issued to senior officials when dealing with the SRI-F, especially the Russians. An interesting effect of the capsule was that it gave the indication of being mildly "buzzed."

Following twenty minutes of mingling with the SRI-F Officers, the dinner bell pinged softly. This alerted everyone to take their seats, and at 1900 hours the first of several courses were served. The initial course was the old Russian staple of a small bowl of hot Borsht, a somewhat bitter soup made primarily with beets, meat, and potatoes.

To cleanse the palate, a small Blini or Russian pancake was served, topped with black sturgeon caviar.

This was followed by a salad called *shuba*, which covers salted herring with layers of grated boiled vegetables, beets, onions and mayonnaise.

This led to the main course of Beef Stroganoff enhanced with Russian sour cream, a variety of mushrooms, and interesting variations of hunting/game meats.

Dessert was a simple honey cake. This delightful dish, the *medovik,* involves alternating ultra-thin layers of honey infused sponge cake and served with sweetened Russian sour cream.

The drink accompanying the dinner was a tea, or *medovukha*, a sweet drink made with fermented-honey, and *kvass*.

Both Americans were highly impressed with the fine meal, and so complimented Admiral Volodin.

"Admiral Volodin," offered Sky King, "this incredible repast has far exceeded anything we might be able to produce aboard an SDF ship. My earnest compliments, sir."

Volodin smile seemed to light up the room at what he was sure were the heartfelt accolades of his SDF guests.

"Sky, oh, please, may I call you Sky?"

"Of course, my friend," said Sky King, "I would be honored."

"Wonderful," bellowed Volodin, and you must call me Nico (Neeko)."

The festivities continued with the normal slate of Russian dancers. By the end of the party, Sky was surprised Volodin hadn't managed to come up with a Russian Dancing Bear.

At precisely 2200 hours, Volodin left the festive atmosphere with the pronouncement that he and his new friend Sky King must retire to his Ready Room for a discussion of somewhat more formal matters. Nico and Sky departed and soon arrived at the Admiral's Ready Room.

Admiral King noticed that the metal flooring of the SRI-F Cruiser was not covered in the rubberized, and far more quiet flooring of SDF ships. The soothing colors covering the passageways of the SDF ships were also missing as the RSN preferred the battleship gray coloring.

Once in Nico's office, he immediately poured two shots of vodka, then placed the bottle on the table, between them.

"Salut, to the making of new friends, and peace throughout the galaxy."

King, of course, had to offer a counter toast before any serious talks could begin. He said, "To the end of strife between our governments. Let us be the catalyst for such a movement."

Both men laughed heartily before Admiral Volodin said, "Admiral King, I thank you for the impressive report prepared for us demonstrating your success in moving this comet. This is a milestone in Earth's history, and I am saddened that the Russian Federation has been unable to assist in this endeavor."

"My friend," said King, while trying to maintain a comradely tone to the meeting, "I completely agree, and I would like to offer this small gift to you. If you are willing, I would be amenable to allow a three-man team, plus yourself aboard the Leyte Gulf. You and your team would be allowed to participate in the operation of one of our one-thousand kWh laser generators during its firing on Holly Thorne.

"In this way, it can be recorded that the RSN did, in fact, have at least a small part in the operation. I believe history will remember this bit of cooperation very well."

For the first time, King realized that Volodin was not only surprised, but moved by this gesture. He was most pleased with the offer.

"I, I don't really know what to say. Of course, I accept, but I must tell you that I would have never considered, for even a second, such a thoughtful gesture on the part of the SDF. Is this offer from you, or from your government?"

"It is from me. I will not discuss it with my government until after the deed is done."

Volodin was, yet again, caught somewhat off balance with this surprising turn of events. He asked, "Will you not be in trouble for such an independent action?"

"Possibly," replied King, "but what can they do, retire me?"

Volodin lowered his head and shook it several times before leveling his eyes on his American counterpart. "Amazing, if I were to do such a thing, the RSN High Command would have me thrown into a Siberian Gulag or spaced. Is what you have just told me the truth?"

"Yes, Nico, you and I come from totally different worlds. That is a truism that saddens me deeply."

Nico quickly turned the conversation in several new directions.

Once the SDF Officers had returned to their Shuttle Craft, Nico thought, *yes, Sky, different worlds indeed. I will be saddened to be the cause of your end, but I have my duty…*

24 OCTOBER 2116
ADMIRAL'S CONFERENCE ROOM
ON STATION ABOARD LEYTE GULF
70,000 MILES PORTSIDE OF HOLLY THORNE

Vice Admiral Perry and Sky King discussed the previous evening's festivities.

King said to his superior, "Sir, I must say that Admiral Volodin is far more congenial and likable than his predecessor, the late Admiral Petrov. He is a magnificent host and puts on a fabulous dinner. He is obviously well educated and culturally refined. His Officers appear to respect and probably fear him. After all, he did Space an Admiral of the Russian Space Navy. That alone gives him lots of street cred.

"His appearance would make an excellent recruitment poster. He is handsome, fit, always composed, and certainly politically savvy. The man-made significant efforts to give me the impression that he has no animosity toward the USUG-C. I could have easily believed in his sincerity.

"Dolph, I swear, I believe that Volodin could drink any other human being under the table. Admiral, this man is dangerous, and I must say that I did not believe much of what he said. I am absolutely convinced that when we have completed our mission with Holly Thorne, the SRI-F Fleet will attack us. I'm not sure how he plans to accomplish this, but I have an idea.

"If I was in his position, I would fire nukes at our comet. I would also conjure up the position that SDF claims of success were untrue. During the attack on Holly, I would also launch a few nukes in our direction, probably ten, one for each ship. The claim would be that pieces of comet destroyed our vessels."

Vice Admiral Perry listened intently and remained silent during Sky's briefing before saying, "Your brief is certainly thorough and most informative, but do you really think the SRI-F would risk war on a planet-wide scale?"

"Dolph, I believe the SRI-F believes they can avoid such a war by utilizing my scenario. Even if they fail, the claim will be that those missiles fired at us was purely accidental. Their apology will be profound. No, sir, I do not think that the SRI-F believes this incident, several hundred million miles from Earth would constitute a USUG-C attack against them."

"Damn, Sky, I wish I could poke holes in your concept, but the scenario does appear sound. I'll take it up with President Greene and the COS. Sky, when do you anticipate the earliest completion of Operation Holly Thorne?"

"Sir, we are convinced that we will reach our goal on or about 15 July 2117. I think the real danger from the SRI-F will occur between the 28th of December and the 1st of January 2118."

Perry said, "Sky, I won't ask if you have a defensive plan because I know that you do. Please enlighten me."

Admiral King said, "Our defensive posture will be to begin reducing our assault on Holly Thorne two days before our announced date of 15 July 2017.

"Sir, since our mission began, Holly Thorne has been throwing large chunks of debris in our general direction. Using the mining vessels, we have focused on converting our laser crews from simple techs to precision gunnery crews. This has had good success. I believe that we have an excellent chance of destroying any missiles directed toward either Holly Thorne or us."

Sky continued saying, "Upon any SRI-F assault against either Holly Thorne or Taffy III, we will immediately turn our one-thousand kWh lasers onto the SRI-F vessels, along with our Phaser Arrays and Railguns. We certainly have the SRI-F Fleet outgunned. If they attack, we will be ready and waiting. Since their attack will come as no surprise, they don't stand a chance against our firepower.

"Upon our return to Earth, I plan to submit a detailed plan to add these large array lasers to our fleet. I will also outline the training program for gunnery crews."

"Sky, you have an excellent plan in place, but I must tell you that destroying the SRI-F Fleet without Presidential approval may not be well received. I have a meeting scheduled with the COS today. Maybe we can get in to see the President then."

"Understood," said Admiral King, "but, sir, no matter what the eventual fallout is, I will not stand down should the SRI-F initiate an attack against us. I also have live, streaming video arrays up and recording each SRI-F ship, so if they do attack, we will have a video proving their treachery."

"I understand and unofficially approve of your plan. I'll be back in touch with you right after my meeting with the President. I feel certain she will approve, but she has to make that call. Keep Taffy III safe, Sky."

"Yes, sir, I will."

"I know you will, Sky. Dolph: Out."

25 OCTOBER 2116
PRESIDENTIAL CONFERENCE ROOM
WHITE HOUSE, WASHINGTON DC

The usual suspects of the Operation Holly Thorne Committee, Mr. Gordon Winters, the NASA Chief, Dr. Tyler Deen, CDC, Vice Admiral Adolphus Perry Commander of the US Space Defense Force, General "Triple H" Howard, Chairman of the Joint Chief's, and Mr. Mack Holland, Chief of Homeland Security milled about the room. They were discussing the destruction of the Chinese Space Cruiser Changsha, and the lack of any response, at all, from the SRI-F. It seemed as though the SRI-F Chairman had elected to ignore the entire issue.

As President Eileen N. Greene entered the room following her Chief of Staff, retired Lieutenant General Harry Wolfe.

"Take your seats, please," said President Greene, as the group quickly found their seats around the Conference Table.

"All right, gentlemen, let's get this show on the road. Gordon, what's new from NASA?"

"Yes, Madame President, thank you. I have just received a report this morning from CIA that they believe the SRI-F has decided that they have no defensible position to blame us for the loss of the Changsha. Therefore, the Intel Community believes that the SRI-F will just ignore the whole situation.

"Our satellite images, which are in your packets, clearly show that the SRI-F Space Force construction sites all seem to indicate vastly speeded up production of new Space Cruisers. I have also noted in the photos, what appear to be new modifications to their vessels. We believe that the SRI-F intends to beef up the armor plating on the hulls, and as you can see, they are adding additional rail-gun blister arrays.

"Additionally, it is clear, from our humint that they have developed a new shielding technology. Madame President, I believe it is time to add this enhancement to our current ships. The secret is apparently out, and if we fail to install this shielding system, our ships will be sitting ducks. We have had the technology for some time but did not wish to install it until the SRI-F developed the technology."

The President interrupted and asked, "Gordon, I was made aware of this at the morning security brief, but I allowed you to restate it for the rest of the committee. What I should have asked this morning, but didn't, is; were we aware that our enemies had developed this technology?"

"Ma'am, I do not have that information, and therefore, anything I might offer is pure speculation. Ultimately, no matter how they obtained this technology, they do have it, and we had better install our own version," replied NASA.

"Admiral Perry, are you prepared to make the appropriate modifications?" asked the President.

"Yes, Madame President, we are able to add the shield generators on station. The generators, themselves are of a relatively compact design. DARPA has assured me that it will take less than a week to complete the shield upgrades."

"Excellent," said President Greene, "please proceed with the installations. It is a pity, though, that we will be unable to have them installed on the Holly Thorne Fleet."

"Yes, Madame President, but neither can our enemies upgrade their vessels opposing Taffy III," added the Chief of Staff.

Greene smiled and thanked NASA for an excellent briefing. She then turned her attention to Dr. Tyler Deen, the CDC Director. "Dr. Deen, are your plans in place, and prepped for the possible pandemic headed our way?"

"Yes, Madame President, we have ultra-hardened our level 5 facilities. The proposed staff have all been notified and have agreed to the assignment. I have also maintained regular contact with Fort Detrick. The Army Corps of Engineers has also added significant landline communications should the normal forms of commo fail. I am confident that our preparations will be completed before Holly Thorne reaches us in only seventeen months."

"Thank you, Doctor, please keep the COS up to date on each phase of your mission preps."

"Of course, Madame President."

"Admiral Perry," said President Greene to Vice Admiral Adolphus Perry the Commander of the US Space Defense Force, "What have you to report to us on this day? Good news, I hope?"

"Madame President, as always seems to be the case, I bear both good and not so good news. In case anyone here is unaware of the latest developments in Operation HT; Admiral Petrov reportedly suffered a massive stroke while in conference with the Senior Captain of the SRI-F Fleet, Captain (P) Nicolay Volodin.

"We believe, however, that upon Petrov's arrival aboard the RSN Soyuz, he was immediately taken into custody and executed by being sucked out of an air-lock. Captain Volodin was, some seventy-minutes later promoted to the rank of Admiral and given command of the SRI-F Fleet.

"Admiral King and Captain Jessica Flynn, Commander of the SDF Cruiser Leyte Gulf, were invited to attend a promotion party for Admiral Nicolay Volodin, who replaced the late Admiral Petrov. Admiral King reported that Volodin is quite the engaging man. His photo and bona-fides are in your packets.

"Following the party, Admiral King reported that he is convinced that the new SRI-F Admiral will declare that Operation Holly Thorne has failed and then he will launch nuclear missiles at the comet and at Taffy III to reduce our Space Combat Force by 70%. If Volodin is successful, he will claim that Taffy III was destroyed by cometary fragments."

President Greene interrupted and asked, "Admiral, do you believe that this Volodin character is capable of pulling off this Act of War against the United States, the United Kingdom, and Germany?"

"No, ma'am, I believe that Admiral King is well prepared for just such a maneuver from the SRI-F Fleet. One of Admiral King's fleet adjustments has been to train the Laser Technicians to be top notch Gunnery Crews.

"His plan is to vastly reduce the laser firings against Holly Thorne, and re-aim them at the SRI-F Vessels. Their mission is two-fold; first to destroy the enemy fleet, then engage the slower moving nuclear missiles. A 1,000-kWh laser generated beam will slice through the enemy ships with incredible ease. This coupled with the simple fact that lasers are a form of light. Their bursts will reach their targets in less than one second.

"Admiral King's plan to defend the comet and his Taffy III fleet is sound. Madame President I hope that you will approve this scenario as King proposes. If he must wait for your approval, Taffy III will be destroyed, and Holly Thorne will become Mount Everest sized rocks which could strike both the Earth and Luna.

"Ma'am, no matter whether you approve King's plan or not, I do not, for one second, believe that he will allow his command and Holly Thorne to be destroyed. He will, like the great commander and tactician that he is, destroy his attacker. I not only support his plan, but I also will not attempt to dissuade him from acting on behalf of his fleet."

President Greene took her famous position of placing her steepled fingers in front of her mouth and tapping the two index fingers as she considered the dilemma before her. After a few seconds, Greene said, "Admiral Perry, I approve of Admiral King's plan, and I want that decision to be plain to each of you around this table. Is there any discussion on this issue?"

Greene looked around the table and into the eyes of each member of the Holly Thorne Committee. The Chief of Staff turned his eyes to the President and said, "Madame President, your decision is sound. My only comment is to suggest that the USUG-Confederation put out a media blitz on the success of Operation HT. I suggest we get the PR Office on board immediately following this meeting. We must try to keep the SRI-

F off balance. I also agree with Admiral Perry, in that the SRI-F Fleet will attack as soon as the mission is complete. May I bring the PR Office on board?"

The President was enthusiastic about the PR Blitz and ordered the COS to proceed. Now, the President of the United States released a deep sigh. She hadn't realized that she had been holding her breath. She smiled and looked to General "Triple H" Howard and asked him to bring everyone up to speed on the progress concerning the Ranger Battalions and their families who would take up residence in the Mount Weather Bunker.

"Thank you, Madame President. I am pleased to announce that the preparations for the Ranger Battalions and their families are ready to be put into operation."

"Excellent," smiled the President.

Mack Holland, Chief of Homeland Security was up next, and the President asked, "Mack, how are the preps going for Mount Weather and Cheyenne Mountain?"

"Madame President, the stocking of supplies in both facilities is going very well. There has, of course, been a somewhat significant uptick in the number of service vehicles in and out of both facilities. We are trying to downplay this issue by utilizing several vendors. We hope that this tactic will help keep the talk down. One service with a huge upswing of deliveries could cause unwanted attention."

The COS asked, "Mack, what more remains to be shipped?"

Mack Holland said, "I'm afraid that we are nowhere near completion of the necessary items. However, I am confident that we will be finished well before our drop-dead date.

"Just food alone for a group of more than two-thousand people for up to four years is a staggering amount. We've had construction crews adding to the facilities at Mount Weather. These additions will house some fairly massive greenhouses and a large rabbit ranch to provide fresh meat and fertilizer. Then comes clothing requirements for the civilians and uniforms for the military contingent. Sanitary products, TP, water access, vehicles, weapons, ammunition, diesel fuel to run the generators for four years, and that is far from all. Fortunately, the cold fusion plants were already up and running."

"Yes," said the COS, "I see your point. I tell you, Mack, I do not envy you this job, and, I'm sorry, but I have to ask, how will you select women's clothing?" This caused everyone to chuckle, but Mack attempted to remain serious. Ultimately, he failed miserably.

Mack also laughed as he said, "Sir, we have decided to provide jumpsuits in all possible sizes. The civilians can have them in whatever color they want, as long as they want dark blue."

"Mack," said the President, "let's back up on that issue and provide several colors of jumpsuits. We can use them to identify differing job types."

"Yes, Madame President, I should have thought of that myself. What is your personal preference for Government attire?"

Eileen said, "I don't really have a preference, other than we exclude pink. I just think it would be good for morale if everyone isn't wearing the exact same color. If you are unable to find sufficient colors, then you might try white and get a lot of dye."

"Yes, ma'am, I'll get right on it."

CHAPTER ELEVEN

NOVEMBER 2117

The U.S. Presidential Election saw President Greene reelected by a landslide. The Legislative Elections, however, did not fare quite so well. Many of the newly elected members of both Houses were from what the media called the Jesus Coalition. They were to be sworn into office on March 10, 2118.

Saudi Arabia, Egypt, Jordan, and Bahrain, had all agreed to the premise of Israel's right to exist some seventy-five years before. Now, these Muslim nations not only fully recognized Israel as a nation but formed an anti-Iranian Pact with their, now friendly, Zionist neighbor.

The world seemed to settle into a period of relative calm as the comet, Holly Thorne became visible to the naked eye. The months raced by.

The Holly Thorne mission was progressing as planned. The SRI-F, though downplayed the progress of Operation HT. They did remain close enough to monitor progress. Admiral's King and Volodin appeared to become fast friends and visited each other's ships regularly.

The world had settled back into the normal everyday existence.

81 Days to Holly Thorne

15 DECEMBER 2117
OVAL OFFICE
WHITE HOUSE, WASHINGTON DC

President Greene had just finished a long and difficult meeting with the "loyal opposition" and was exhausted. She stood to stretch her legs, then opened the door to the outer office.

She said, "Tessa, please get the COS, (ret General Wolfe), Admiral Perry, General Howard, Mr. Gordon Winter, and Mr. Mack Holland on my schedule for 3:15 this afternoon and cancel all of my remaining appointments for the day."

"Yes, ma'am, I'll get right on it," replied the President's Secretary.

At 3:15 pm the COS, Admiral Perry, General Howard, Mr. Gordon Winter, and Mr. Mack Holland were ushered into the Presidential Conference Room.

The President entered the room one minute later. "Gentlemen, please take a seat."

Once everyone was seated, President Eileen Greene, as usual, cut right to the crux of this ad-hoc meeting. "As I am sure you all know, the SRI-F has, this very morning, countered our publicity blitz with one of their own. Theirs, of course, claims that the mission to move Holly Thorne has actually been a complete failure. My friends, this can only be the prelude to the attack which Admiral Perry warned us about just a few months ago. Admiral Perry, would you please share your thoughts on this new development?"

"Yes, Madame President, of course. I am in complete agreement with your estimate. The SRI-F is, unquestionably, preparing to attack and destroy our fleet. They will use this lie about the failure of Operation HT as a ruse. We can expect tensions to rise over the next few days. I anticipate their attack will commence somewhere between 28 January and 1 February."

"Thank you, Admiral, now General Howard; your thoughts?"

"Madame President, I can only add that if Admiral Perry is correct, and I am sure that he is, we must increase our Def-Con status to at least Level 3. I would also suggest that you contact the SRI-F Chairman, personally, and make it clear to him that firing missiles at our comet could lead to a global tragedy."

"Thank you, General. All right, let's shift gears just a bit. Mack, please tell us that you are nearing completion of stocking Mount Weather."

"Madame President," said Mr. Mack Holland, the Chief of Homeland Security, "I am pleased to say that we will complete this mission within the next ten days, guaranteed."

"Now, that, my friends, is truly wonderful news," said a somewhat relieved President Greene.

16 DECEMBER 2117
CNN NEWS
LONDON OFFICE

A panel of four talking heads sat behind an elevated plexiglass desk. They were discussing the SRI Federation claims that the USUG

Confederation was falsifying data to show that Holly Thorne's trajectory realignment was nearly complete.

The Russian's produced a video demonstrating their contention that the actual path of this monster comet was boring down upon the Earth. The SRI-F pledged to destroy the comet Holly Thorne if the USUG Confederation proved to not be up to the task of safely removing her.

CNN then ran the SRI-F video, produced quite elegantly by RT (Russian TV) News Network. This vid which purported to prove that the massive comet, Holly Thorne, had not, in fact, been altered at all. The RT film then portrayed a computerized image of the destruction of all life on Earth should this comet strike our planet.

The panel of talking heads accepted the RT film as proof that the United States, the United Kingdom, and Germany had failed miserably in their effort to move the comet. This failure, the panel decided, placed the Earth and Luna in the crosshairs of Holly Thorne.

Within twenty-four hours, this roundtable discussion managed to convince nearly one-half of the world's population that the SRI-F version of events was true, as opposed to the USUG-C's claims of successfully altering the comet's path.

The members of the panel had sided with the SRI-F and their proclamation that the USUG-C, specifically the government of President Eileen Greene, had placed the Earth and Luna in potentially dire straits.

The RT News Network also parroted the CNN reports. These two quasi-news outlets fed off each other and were soon followed by socialist networks from around the planet. World opinion quickly began to slip away from the USUG-C, as only two major news outlets, FOX and the German Station WELT TV openly supported the USUG-C contention that all was well with the Holly Thorne mission.

Around the world, protests began to spring up in support of the SRI-F position and demanded that the USUG-C withdraw to allow the SRI-F Fleet to destroy the comet.

1 FEBRUARY 2118
ON STATION
50,000 MILES PORTSIDE OF HOLLY THORNE

The USUG-C Crewmen grew ever more pensive as the attack, which had been anticipated between 28 January and today, 1 February had not come. Each member of Taffy III knew that the SRI-F would soon attack, but tension or no, they were ready and eager to end the fight.

Admiral King and Captain Flynn enjoyed breakfast in the Captain's Ready Room.

Captain Ward sat in his Ready Room having breakfast and watching a video feed showing the SRI-F Cruisers. In just a nanosecond the video screen displayed the launch of dozens of missiles exiting their silos on the SRI-F ships.

Captain Ward jumped to his feet, spilling a carafe of coffee onto the floor. Klaxons began echoing throughout the SDF Fleet. RED ALERT: MISSILES INBOUND. Spacers rushed to their Battle Stations.

On board the USSN Astrid, Phobos, and Deimos, the laser gunnery crews were fully manned with lasers pre-ranged and sighted in on the six Cruisers of the SRI-F Fleet. At only twenty-thousand miles from the SRI-F, the 1,000 kWh Lasers simply could not miss.

Captain Ward rushed to the Bridge as the Klaxons continued their ahoogha wailing. As he rushed through the door to the Bridge, he shouted, "Open fire!" Taking his Command Chair, Ward demanded, "XO, status, and shut off those damned klaxons!"

"Aye, sir, as per your orders our laser gunners opened fire on their assigned SRI-F targets immediately upon sensor detection of the missiles being launched by the SRI-F. Sir, all seven enemy ships were destroyed with the first salvo from our ninety laser batteries. The inbound missiles directed against Taffy III have now also been destroyed. We are currently systematically destroying the sixty missiles fired at the comet."

"Very well, Number One, were we able to get them all?"

At just that instant the video stream turned white as, at least, one SRI-F missile detonated a thirty-megaton blast which significantly damaged Holly Thorne. The blast sheared off debris in an arc of roughly two-hundred and seventy degrees from the impact point.

The video quickly returned, showing thousands of rocks being hurled out into space. Much of this debris was directed on an unavoidable path toward the three USUG-C mining vessels.

Captain Ward, realizing that he had perhaps only twenty to thirty minutes before the shrapnel struck his ship and that he could not get out of the debris field before the three mining ships were overwhelmed, ordered the ship to roll onto its side. This position only exposed storage and ore bays to the oncoming rocks. Along the ship's bottom were six laser blisters which were at once put into action to destroy as many of the incoming meteors as possible. Phobos and Deimos followed the example of Astrid, to provide the least vulnerable aspect to the incoming meteors. The laser crews did an admirable job, but they were simply flooded by the tsunami of debris.

Admiral King quickly made contact and asked if the Astrid could get out of the way of the debris.

"No, sir, that's not going to be possible. Perhaps if we had an hour, we might have attempted to run, but our computer tells us that the incoming rocks are traveling at speeds of up to ninety-thousand miles per hour. I have ordered our ships to roll onto their sides to expose only storage and ore bays. Still, at those speeds, many hits will go through both sides of our ships. We'll doubtless suffer many casualties. All we can do is hold tight and hope for the best.

"Admiral, I hope you have turned the fleet and are under full thrust at a forty-five-degree oblique angle. You may be able to reach safety by getting ahead of the debris path."

King said, "Yes, Al, we have done exactly that. I believe we'll make it. Our scans indicate that the meteor shower will be short-lived. It should last no more than a few seconds for nearly all of Holly's debris to pass. I wish you God's blessings, my friend."

"Thank you, Admiral, a bit of luck headed our way would be a very good thing. Our own scans show that the arc of the meteors headed our way will widen significantly over the fifty-thousand miles from the comet. That spreading arc may save us. Still, there is a lot of crap heading directly at us. The Gunnery Crews are already engaged, but it will be a close thing. I'll contact you as soon as this wall of rocks has passed."

The pieces of Holly Thorne approached the three ships as though fired from a shotgun and all three vessels suffered significant hull breaches. Over three-hundred crewmen died from both explosive decompression and being struck by the comet's fragments.

God's blessing was, in fact, with the three mining ships as none of the giant meteor pieces struck home, thanks to the excellent gunnery of the laser crews. The remainder of the SDF fleet was able to get ahead of the debris and were able to avoid being struck.

Once hull repair crews were dispatched both inside and to the outer hulls, Captain Ward contacted his Admiral with status updates and damage reports.

"Sir," said Captain Ward, "Captains Chen and Putin report similar damage to that of the Astrid; many hull breaches by small meteors. They will forward full reports to you as soon as the information is available. We got lucky, sir, very lucky. We anticipate forming back up and making way to Mars within the next couple of hours.

"Admiral, I don't think I can ever express how truly thankful I am that you were the man in charge, or how pleased I am to have had the honor to serve with you. Godspeed, sir, I am, and always will be, your friend."

Sky King felt humbled by Captain Alan Ward's words and responded in like manner, adding that he hoped that the two might one day serve together yet again.

1 FEBRUARY 2118
PRESIDENT'S CONFERENCE ROOM
WHITE HOUSE
1600 PENNSYLVANIA AVE,
WASHINGTON, DC, USA

The President of the United States of America, Mrs. Eileen N. Greene entered the Conference Room and directed everyone present to take their seats. She then convened the meeting and began with Admiral Perry.

"Madame President, just an hour ago the SRI-F Fleet attacked both the comet and the USUG-C Fleet with nuclear-tipped missiles, just as

Admiral King had predicted. The SRI-F Fleet fired sixty nuclear-tipped missiles at Holly Thorne, and ten additional missiles at the USUG-C Fleet.

"Admiral King was prepared for this possibility, and within two seconds of confirmation of the SRI-F missile firing, the Mining Vessels made short work of the SRI-F Fleet. As King had predicted the laser fire took out the entire SRI-F Fleet in less than a second. Unfortunately, one missile did get through to Holly Thorne. This single blast broke a portion of the comet into thousands of fragments. Hundreds struck the hulls of the three mining vessels. None of the ships were destroyed, and repair crews were able to repair the damage within a few hours. Casualties were two-hundred and thirty crewmen, two, of which, were part of the EVA repair crews."

The President's Secretary burst into the Oval Office and said, "Madame President, the Chairman of the SRI Federation is on the phone. He sounds near panic and wishes to speak with you immediately."

The call was forwarded to the President's phone, which she placed on speaker so everyone could hear the conversation. "Madame President," said, Chairman Alexi Belinsky, "I have just learned of the horrible situation at the Holly Thorne site. This action was not sanctioned by anyone in the SRI Federation. This attack against Holly Thorne was solely the responsibility of the newly promoted Admiral Volodin. As I am sure you know, our entire fleet was destroyed by the debris from the comet.

"I am making this call to ensure that you do not take any action which could plunge our planet into a global war. As you know, the SRI Federation seeks only peace and equity with the USUG-Confederation. We, therefore, want you to know that we hold no ill will against the

USUG-C. We hope that, by this call, and the fact that our alert status has been lowered to Def Con 1, that you will do the same and we can avoid war."

"Mr. Chairman, I deeply appreciate your communication and your acceptance of responsibility for this disaster. I, tentatively, agree to a military stand-down and I will communicate with you again following talks with our allies. Until then, I insist that all construction of SRI-F Spacecraft be halted until the completion of our future discussions. Are we in agreement on this interim issue?"

"What? Why? How could you even ask for such a thing? No, this is impossible. I cannot agree to such a proposal, no, never."

"Alexi, let's stop the posturing and talk sensibly. You are certainly aware of the USUG Cruisers above each of the SRI-F Capitals. I have ordered those Warships to redeploy to the construction sites of your military shipbuilding facilities. If construction continues, I will order those facilities destroyed.

"My friend, you must know that your agreement on this condition will go far in proving that you are a peace-loving Federation. Failure to comply will result in the destruction of those facilities. Alexi, I implore you to cease construction in this tension-filled time. Let us seek a peaceful resolution. We mean you no harm. Are we agreed?"

Sounding utterly deflated, Belinsky said, "President Greene, I accept your conditions. I will direct our allies to follow suit, but if they cheat, please do not blame peace-loving Russia."

"Alexi, I agree, in principle, with your proposal. I certainly hope you can be sufficiently forceful in consultations with your allies.

"Item two, you must immediately, as in the next sixty minutes reverse your ridiculous posturing over her change of orbit. Alexi, this is not negotiable. Admit that your statements were false about Holly Thorne. I don't care who you blame for the incorrect information, but you now have fifty-nine minutes before we strike your spaceship construction sites and your space station."

Belinsky attempted to interrupt but was literally shushed by President Greene.

"No, do not interrupt. I told you this is not negotiable: fifty-nine minutes Belinsky, no more."

The Chairman knew he was beaten, and also knew that he had to work to gain time and distance from this tragic end to the SRI-F plan to destroy the USUG Fleet.

"Madame President, I agree to your terms and pledge to find the fools who provided such erroneous information concerning the comet."

Both parties were greatly relieved as they said their farewells. Greene then hung up the phone, ending the conversation.

"Admiral Perry," said Greene, "have our Space Navy keep a close eye on those construction sites."

President Greene looked to Admiral Perry and said, "Gus, from the destruction unleashed by our 1,000 kWh lasers, it appears that the days of enhanced armor are over. We must quickly update our fleet with multiple shield generators. Is it possible to develop wide angled laser bursts?"

Admiral Perry tapped a pencil lightly against his notepad before he answered. "Madame President, lasers are very narrow focused beams. To spread them out reduces their power to the point of that of a flashlight. So, no ma'am, DARPA does not believe that wide angled lasers are possible.

"Admiral King and I were discussing this same issue, just yesterday, and I believe that he has come up with a potential way to achieve the same effect, without degradation of the power of the laser. He said that upon his return he would like to try an old US Air Force technique.

"Back in the late twentieth century, an automated tail gun was added to the legendary B-52 Bomber. This mini-gun, which fired six-thousand round per minute, produced a rope of rounds and because it fired so fast, the Air Force found it difficult to achieve any dispersal at all. After much brainstorming and mental gear grinding, the idea of adding a shaking device to the mini-gun proved to be the answer. The rope of bullets became a moderate spray. The idea was simple but ingenious. Admiral Perry believes the principle of Occam's Razor may also vastly improve the destructive power of our laser weapons."

"Occam's Razor?" asked Mack Holland.

Admiral Perry smiled and said, "Mack, Occam was an ancient Arabic Mathematician who said that the simplest solution to a problem was usually the best. Today, we call it the Kiss Principal, or Keep It Simple, Stupid."

The group spent the next hour discussing both the call from Belinsky and the possible ramifications concerning the total destruction of the SRI-F Space Fleet. The COS was directed to inform his Russian counterpart that the SRI-F had twelve hours to cease all construction of military space vessels. Following this vibrant discussion, Mr. Winters was asked by President Greene to present his portion of the briefing.

Mr. Gordon Winters said, "Thank you, Madame President. Gordon got to his feet and walked to a seventy-five-inch computer screen. He touched the screen and indicated a point, placing the mining ships of the SDF Fleet one-month past the orbit of Mars.

"Madame President," said Gordon, "with Operation HT now complete, our SDF Fleet will return to Earth. Once rudimentary hull repairs have been made, the three mining vessels will depart for the Mars, Red Sands facility where the repairs will be inspected for possible weaknesses."

The President asked, "What is the status of Admiral King? Will he remain on active duty or return to the Astrid?"

Admiral Perry spoke up and said, "Ma'am, I have asked Admiral King to remain on active service, and he has graciously accepted. I have also sent a request to promote Admiral King to three stars and that he be placed in charge of the Fleet upgrades, refits, and initial command of a new Training Command. Madame President, I hope you will second my request."

The President looked at Admiral Perry and said, "I will, of course, second your recommendation, but I must ask why you would want to take such a capable tactician out of command of the fleet? Come on, Gus, tell us your nefarious plan; out with it."

Perry smiled broadly and responded with, "Madame President, my plan is hardly nefarious. It is my plan for him to return to space in command of the SDF Fleet once the ships are ready to see action and the training of crews is complete. At that point, the Training Command will be given to Admiral Lantz Ogden. You are, as always, absolutely correct that our Admiral King belongs in space leading our fleet."

Everyone around the table took great pleasure in the Vice Admiral's plan, for none could argue that Admiral Sky King deserved anything less.

"Thank you, Gus, you have my complete support of this plan, and the Confederation also thanks you for having the foresight to have the right man in the job."

8 FEBRUARY 2118
ABOARD THE MINING VESSEL ASTRID
EN ROUTE TO RED SANDS, MARS STATION

The three ships which had successfully pushed Holly Thorne aside from her path toward Earth were enroute to Mars. The atmosphere among the crew was electric as the realization that they were all now, very rich men. The majority of the spacers kept their desire to leave the service of Krupp, Gmbh and live out the remainder of their lives in luxury fooled no one. Captain Ward, knew that Krupp would need to take on new crews. In fact, he had contacted Admiral King, seeking continued service with the US Space Defense Force. Ward's mentor had assured him that his application would be accepted and that following a crash course at the Space Academy, he would become Captain of the first new Cruiser to be completed.

As Captain Ward returned to his quarters, he felt a bit flushed, and a somewhat persistent cough had begun during the night. Now, some three hours after speaking with Admiral King, he realized that he was running a temperature. He rose from his desk and immediately heard, what appeared to be the entire Bridge Crew coughing.

Ward quickly made his way to the infirmary and discovered a long line waiting to see the Medical Personnel. Each man had a breather over his mouth.

As the crew realized that the Captain was among them, someone shouted, "Captain on deck, make way!"

The crewmen stood against the wall allowing the Captain to pass. Upon entering the small infirmary, the first Doctor he came to immediately gave Alan a breathing mask and demanded that he put it on.

Captain Ward asked the Doctor if he had any idea of what was happening.

"No, sir, I do not," answered the Doctor, "and I mean no disrespect, but I do not have time to discuss it with you, sir."

The Med Staff was frustrated and at a loss as to what must be done, other than record temperatures, hand out sleep aids and order the sick to their quarters.

Alan gave the Doctor some space and began a walkthrough inspection of the ship. At every turn, he found very sick crewmen. It quickly became obvious to him that one-hundred percent of his crew was ill and unable to perform their duties. Alan could not fathom how nearly twelve-thousand spacers could become so ill, so fast, and all at once.

Returning to his Ready Room, Ward announced to the crew that all functions were to be placed on auto and ordered all crewmen who were ill to their quarters.

He then spoke with Master Chief Karson and directed him to power up the servo-bots that were primarily for emergencies in the fusion stations. Karson was ordered to reprogram them to deliver meals and water to every crewman on the ship.

Chief Karson said, "Sir, everyone here is sick, but I didn't realize that the entire crew was infected. I hate to admit it, sir, but I am feeling weaker by the moment, so I'll get right on reprogramming the servo-bots."

"Thank you, Chief," said the Captain.

It was now some six hours since Ward had awakened with a cough and he was exhausted. He made one last visit to an empty Bridge and attempted to contact the Phobos and Deimos with no luck. He then contacted Admiral King.

"Sir, every man aboard is very ill, myself included. I have lost all communications with my sister ships, so I must assume they are in the same situation. I have ordered the Astrid placed on the automated systems and the crew to their quarters. My guess is that we have, somehow, become ill with a virulent form of influenza. I have only one guess as to how this pathogen entered our ships. Holly Thorne has a flu bug, and it is a pisser. As soon as I sign-off with you, I will make one last call to Red Sands, informing them of our condition."

Admiral King responded with, "You have taken the correct steps, now go to bed and I pray you will get well soon. Don't worry about contacting Red Sands, I will see to that. Get lots of rest Al. I'll speak with you again upon your recovery."

Captain Ward managed to drag himself to his quarters and into bed. He quickly fell into a troubled sleep.

During his illness, it was all he could do to eat, drink, and drag himself to the toilet. Ward's temperature seemed to hold at 103°. For seven days he had no idea if anyone was still alive aboard the Astrid. Alan would not have been surprised at his own death. Every muscle in his body ached as though they were being stretched like rubber-bands that were clamped on each end, well beyond their normal length. His head pounded as if a base drum tried to work its way out of his brain. Delirium was now the normal state of existence.

16 FEBRUARY 2118
ABOARD THE MINING VESSEL ASTRID
EN ROUTE TO RED SANDS, MARS STATION

On day eight, Captain Ward was finally able to sit up without the overwhelming dizziness he had known for the past week. He considered getting dressed but found that the effort to go to the toilet was still too exhausting to allow any frivolous exercise, like dressing. Ward continued to force himself to eat, drink, lean on the bulkhead to visit the toilet and sleep.

The hundreds of servo-bots continued to make the rounds to every set of quarters, leaving some kind of tasteless blocks of high caloric and vitamin enriched jello-like food. At least he assumed it was food. Alan was glad that the food cubes also contained, anti-diarrhea and pain relievers, though he could not imagine how bad the pain would have been without them.

Day nine brought hope that he might actually survive this incredibly debilitating illness. For the first time in nine days of misery, Captain Alan Ward was actually able to take a shower and brush his teeth. This small victory, however, proved to be the limit of his endurance. He thought, *tomorrow I will get dressed and make some rounds.* He knew those rounds would not take him far from his cabin, but it was a start.

Ward awoke on day ten, 18 February and felt surprisingly better. The dizziness was gone, and for the first time since the onset of the flu, Alan felt hungry, *no,* he thought, *more like ravenous.*

As he arose from his bed, Alan realized that he felt almost normal. There was no dizziness, nausea, and most noticeably, no pain, anywhere. His muscles were relaxed, and the bass drum had marched its way out of his head. He realized that the only remaining symptom was an overall weakness of both body and mind.

The Captain of the Astrid made his way into the passageway and was assaulted by the stench of death. The odor was so powerful that the automated air filters could not contain it. *Am I the only survivor?* Ward wondered.

Still in Officer Country, Alan made his way to his XO's cabin. He knocked and receiving no answer, Alan opened the door and saw the decaying corpse of his friend and Executive Officer Darryl Barnes. The XO had fallen while trying to make his way to the toilet. Barnes did not have the strength to get up, and there he died, alone and miserably ill.

After checking to make sure the XO was dead, Captain Ward continued to the cabin shared by LT Peter Proud and LT Logan. Both men were awake and at the Captain's knock said, in unison, "Come."

As the Captain entered the cabin, both men began to rise, but Alan ordered them to remain sitting. Like their Captain, both men were still a bit shaky but felt remarkably better. They ensured the Captain that they would be back on duty within the hour.

"Pete," said the Captain, "I want a tally of who is alive. The XO is dead, so until we find someone senior, I want you to fill in as XO. Can do?"

"Yes, sir can do, sir."

"Logan, find Chiefs Harkins and Karson. If they are up and about have them report to me at their earliest convenience. I'll be on the Bridge going over the ship's automated logs."

"Yes, sir," said LT Logan, I'll get right on it, sir. Oh, would it be all right if I showered first, I'm pretty smelly right now."

For the first time in ten days, Captain Ward actually caught himself smiling as he said, "Yes, LT, I highly recommend that course of action. Now, listen up. My guess is that we are going to find that possibly thousands of crew members did not make it, so prepare yourselves. Roger?"

Both men said in unison, "Roger that, sir."

"All right then, I'll be on the Bridge," said Ward as he closed the door and made his way forward to the Command Bridge.

Ward found that his strength was returning rapidly and was hungrier than ever. Hunger forced him to delay his trip to the Bridge as he made his way to the Ship's Mess. Upon his arrival, he discovered that three of the ships forty cooks were already there. The smell of brewing coffee and the sight of sandwiches stacked on trays brought a sense of delight and well-being that was only out-matched by the taste of said coffee and sandwiches.

Ward asked the cooks about survivors in their area. The men didn't know exactly how many, but they said that most had died. The others would report for duty after they showered and dressed.

"Cap'n, we didn't really know what to do, so we just came on in and started some coffee and something for the crew to eat."

Captain Ward looked at these three men with immense pride as he said, "Men, I am so proud of you. What you are doing here will spread throughout the ship. Others will follow your lead, thank you."

As the Captain turned to resume his trek to the Bridge, his attendant, Yoeman Penny Prichard entered the Mess and upon seeing the Captain walked up to him with a small smile. She said, "Captain, I am so happy to see that you came through. Is there anything I can do for you?"

Ward smiled and said, "Yes, Penny, get something to eat then report to LT Logan. Assist him in finding out how many of us are still alive."

The Yoeman said, "Yes, sir, I'll just grab some coffee and a sandwich to take with me."

"No," said her Captain, "you will sit down to eat before you begin your mission. I'm also pretty sure that L Ts Logan and Proud will come in to find something to eat in just a few minutes."

"Aye, aye, sir, thank you, Captain."

Ward was only on the Bridge for a couple of minutes before both Chief Harkins and Karson reported for duty. Alan directed both men to seats and said, "Kit, job two for you is to get the filtering system repaired and then begin a system's update. I hope that we'll find things, for the most part, are running fine, but the air filters have me concerned. Roger?"

"Yes, sir, of course," replied Chief Kit Karson, "but you said job two. What is job one?"

Ward smiled and asked, "Chief, have you had any coffee or something to eat, yet?"

"Oh, no, sir, that can wait. I'll get right on the filters before I eat."

"No, Chief, the filters are job two. I am telling you that before you start on your many tasks, you and Chief of the Boat Harkins will get some solid food, and coffee into your systems. Am I clear, here?"

Chief Karson started to protest, but the Chief of the Boat cut him off saying, "Kit, shut your pie hole, and follow your Captain's orders. I don't want to be forced to haul your sorry old ass up before the Captain's Mast."

Kit looked contrite and just nodded his head before saying, "Will do, sir."

"Good, now, Chief Harkins, job two for you is to form up a detail to start policing up the bodies. Put them in one of the loading bays and bring the temp down to freezing, then report back to me. That task may take several days."

"Aye, sir," replied Chief Harkins, "it just might, at that."

"Okay, then, let's get to it. Oh, if you see any officers up and around, send them to the Bridge. You may commandeer anyone else, except for the cooks, to complete your missions. Hourly updates, gentlemen, hourly updates."

Both Chiefs said, "Aye, sir," and headed for the Mess Hall.

18 FEBRUARY 2118, 1535 HOURS
ABOARD THE MINING VESSEL ASTRID
EN ROUTE TO RED SANDS, MARS STATION

"Leyte Gulf: Astrid: Over."

The Leyte Gulf responded almost immediately.

"Astrid: Leyte Gulf: hear you five by five, how me? Over."

"Five by five, this is Captain Ward. Is Admiral King available?"

"Aye, sir, wait: Out."

Within a couple of minutes, Admiral King arrived at the USSN Leyte Gulf's Communication Station. He was extremely relieved to hear that Captain Ward had finally recovered.

Before taking the mic, King instructed JJ to record the conversation with Captain Ward.

Yes, sir, of course, replied JJ.

"Alan," said Admiral Sky King, "it is so good to hear from you. How are you feeling?"

"Much better, sir," said Captain Alan Ward, "thank you, surprisingly, my strength is returning very quickly. I don't really understand why, but I am happy about it. Sir, it's good to be able to contact you.

"Admiral, I am loathe to tell you, but the death toll from this flu may stretch into the thousands. I have crews out making a count of survivors and policing up the bodies. I have directed that they be placed in an empty loading bay with the temperature set at zero degrees Fahrenheit.

"The odor of death has overwhelmed the air filtering system. Master Chief Karson is working on that now. My XO Darryl Barnes is dead. I have temporarily placed Lieutenant Proud as his temporary replacement until we find out how many Officers pulled through.

"I will provide a complete list as soon as the numbers and names come in. As things stand right now, Admiral, I'm not even sure if we have sufficient crew to run this ship."

Admiral King was aghast at the initial report from his friend, Al Ward. He also quickly realized the potential ramifications for Earth when it passed through Holly Thorne's tail. He again told his friend how happy he was to learn of the flu's passing.

"Thank you, Captain. Please keep us updated with each new discovery."

Ward said, "Yes, Admiral, I'll keep you apprised of our progress as we discover exactly where we stand. I'll also transmit a copy of the computer logs that were recorded during the last ten days. Sky, some parts of the video recordings are painful to watch."

Following the initial brief from Captain Ward, King returned to his Ready Room to contact Vice Admiral Perry.

"Wake up, JJ."

Yes, Sky, how may I help?

"JJ, transmit your data to Admiral Perry's AI. Also, send a message via regular channels requesting a meeting."

Done, I would guess that we will hear from the Admiral shortly.

Sky sat before his personal computer and began forming his briefing to Vice Admiral Adolphus Perry.

Two hours later, JJ alerted Sky that Admiral Perry was connected via his AI.

"Sir," said Admiral King, "just two hours ago I spoke with Captain Ward of the Mining Vessel Astrid. He has informed me that the loss of lives aboard the Astrid, Phobos, and Deimos appears to be huge." King went on to give his friend Admiral Perry the total information available.

"Sir, I suggest you meet with the President and prepare her for the pandemic which, I believe is irrevocably bearing down upon Earth. I will keep you up to date with new information, as it comes in. What say we keep this line open for now? Dolph, please make sure my Hermie is safe. I'm counting on you."

Admiral Perry assured Sky that his daughter would be safe in the underground city at Mount Weather. She would stay with his wife, Coe and himself.

18 FEBRUARY 2118, 1900 HOURS
OVAL OFFICE
WASHINGTON, DC

Vice Admiral Perry sought an emergency meeting with the President and the Comet Committee. The group arrived for the council at 1900 hours. They gathered in President Greene's Conference Room. Once everyone was seated, President Greene asked Admiral Perry to brief the committee on his conversation with Admiral King.

The Admiral provided the Comet Committee with transcripts as well as downloading them, along with the video to each member's AI.

The video which was downloaded to each of the AIs had been edited to only show the struggles of the crew as they made their way to the toilet. This video also saw many men and women die in the ship's companionways. The video playing in each AI was three dimensional and provided the perspective of the viewer actually standing in those same corridors. They watched as crewmen fell and did not have the strength to get back on their feet. This pitiful scene was replayed possibly thousands of times, however, in the interest of time, most had been edited by Admiral Perry's staff. Once the vid ended, Admiral Perry informed them that there were 423 vids showing the deaths of Spacers on the three Mining Vessels.

The impact of the Admiral's Briefing was heartbreaking, and deeply disturbing. President Greene asked in a low and solemn voice, "CDC, what can you do?"

In an equally low and solemn voice, Dr. Tyler Deen almost whispered, "Nothing, Madame President, absolutely nothing. In twenty-four days, our civilization will come crashing down around our ears, and there is no way to prevent the evil that this way comes."

The President stood and said, "Gentlemen, we need some time to digest the information we have just received. We will reconvene tomorrow, February 19th at 3:00 pm. I hope that you can all bring suggestions to help save us, or at least, ameliorate this catastrophe. Good evening," said the leader of the Free World, as she left the room.

Alone in the Oval Office, Eileen Nearing Greene steepled her fingers under her chin and sat, in silence. Tears ran freely, furrowing her cheeks. Eileen did not want to survive this cleansing of humanity.

She thought, *what would be the point? Why should I survive while three-hundred million other Americans die?*

A soft tap on the door went unanswered. *No, I must be strong, or at least appear to be strong and in control of my emotions.* Eileen ignored whoever wanted something more from her, *more, more, more.* Those people who met with her always wanted some little piece of her. Eileen wanted to scream at that soft rapping on her door; *Leave me alone! I have nothing left to give!*

The door slowly opened and in came her husband, Lamar, The First Gentleman, her husband of forty years. Lamar was a retired Senator from Florida. He whispered into the dark room, "Darling, are you in here?"

"Yes," said Eileen, "I'm here, but I don't think I'm fit company for anyone right now."

Lamar sat beside Eileen on the couch and placing his arm around her, said, "Perhaps, you're not fit for man nor beast right now, and I can only offer a shoulder and the mature love of our forty years together." Lamar then kissed the President of the United States on the forehead.

He eased her onto the backrest, and the two just sat quietly as Lamar lightly stroked her left shoulder which had always been cathartic to Eileen. They sat for nearly an hour before Eileen looked at her loving husband and said, "How is it that you always know when to show up with your shoulder ready for me to lean on?"

Lamar smiled and said, "Well, I guess I must be psychotic, er, psychic." This small bit of humor caused Eileen to chuckle. Quietly, hand-in-hand the two left the Oval Office, followed by the duty Secret Servicemen, and returned to their quarters.

The meeting scheduled for 19 February was canceled after each member sent word that they had found nothing to add. The techno-world was coming to an end, and the President came to the conclusion that she would just have to soldier on.

She met with her Chief of Staff and informed him that if this coming holocaust, this apocalypse, proved to be as bad as the evidence suggested, then civilization would begin again from scratch.

Scientists, scholars, farmers, mechanics, carpenters, along with many other skilled vocations were literally kidnapped, along with their families and secreted to the city under Mount Weather. Only then would they be told of the coming pandemic.

There were, of course, far too many holes left in the list of needed skill sets, but there was too little time and insufficient opportunity to further expand what the President believed would be the new capital of the United States.

18 FEBRUARY 2116, AD
THE DOG AND PONY BAR
MORGANTOWN, WV

The Dog and Pony Bar in Morgantown was old, dark, and busy, especially on Friday and Saturday nights. Two bartenders fought to keep up with orders for those fruity little sissy drinks ordered by the young freshman ladies, accompanied by dates spending Daddy's money. Those customers who had to either work for a living or hold down a job while going to school drank mostly Bud Light or PBR.

Bartenders, John Mills and Gale Storm, were two such students who were working their way through school. No student loans or parents who were either rich or who took out second mortgages on their homes, no, it was work hard now, and the payoff would be down life's dusty road.

Gale was in her second year Master's Program in paleontology and would graduate in May. She had applied for a Spring position on a dig in the Moundsville, West Virginia area, where it was hoped that the dig would finally shed some light on the identity of those ancient and unknown Mound Builders.

She felt fairly sure that she would be selected for the paid position as she had been on three previous digs. Her last posting had been as an Assistant Team-leader on a dig team that made several new discoveries concerning the Viking settlements in Eastern Canada.

22 FEBRUARY 2118
ABOARD THE ASTRID
EN ROUTE TO RED SANDS, MARS

"Leyte Gulf: Astrid: Get Admiral King on the horn, now: Over."

"Roger Astrid: Wait: Out."

Within one moment Admiral King took the mike. "Astrid: King: Over."

"Admiral," said Captain Ward, "At the 0600 change of the watch, it was discovered that many duty personnel did not report for their scheduled duty station. Upon inspection of the ship's crew quarters, we have discovered that roughly 50% of the crew has just disappeared. They have gone into hiding, and on ships this size, with our skeleton crews, there are thousands of places for crewmen to hide. Sir, I have initiated a search, but so far, we have not found a single missing spacer. I will keep you informed as to the search results, but with our limited personnel, I am not hopeful of success."

"Alan, did you have any idea this would happen?"

"No, sir, none, we just woke up this morning and found half of the crew missing."

"All right, Alan, please do keep us up to date."

CHAPTER TWELVE

8 Days to Holly Thorne

26 FEBRUARY 2118
ABOARD THE ASTRID
EN ROUTE TO RED SANDS, MARS

Four days passed without finding a single missing crewman.

Master Chief Karson, after his morning shower, donned a clean uniform and proceeded to his duty station. Karson exited the locker room and turned left toward the lift which would take him to J Deck.

Instead of an empty passageway, Chief Karson found himself facing a heavily built man in a rumpled and dirty uniform.

Karson's last thought was; *Oh, shit…*

The man, who was not quite a man, let out a roar and immediately struck Chief Karson on the head with a wooden club made from a broken 2X4. Kit's brain had only begun to register the power, and pain, of the blow before his skull was damaged to the point of causing death. He was dead before his knees hit the floor.

This scenario was followed throughout the ships as the attackers came out of hiding. Their numbers grew as the former crewmen roamed aimlessly through the companionways and became packs, attacking anyone in their path. Compartment after compartment fell to the relentless onslaught. Every deck held these sub-humans. They were dressed in uniform, but the resemblance to modern Homo Sapiens ended there.

The Raiding Parties roamed, undetected by the Bridge Crew as the fighting began and ended so quickly. This mutiny had remained undetected until the Watch change. When only a very few responded to their duty stations, others were sent out to discover the reason.

It didn't take long for the searchers to begin finding the evidence of the attacks. Lieutenant Peter Proud came upon a fight in progress on A Deck and immediately reported his findings to the Bridge.

"Captain," whispered a frightened, Lieutenant Proud, into his communicator, "we are under attack by an alien force. Sir, they look like cavemen, but they are dressed in our uniforms."

Proud remained around an intersecting companionway and every few seconds he would peek around to report on the progress of the fight. With his back against the wall, Proud reported, "Sir, the aliens appear to be very strong and very quick. They seem to communicate only with primordial grunts and howls of rage. Their heads appear to be square along with the eye sockets."

"Pete, what type of weapons are they using?"

"Sir, they are using fists and clubs. I have not seen any modern weapons. Let me take a quick look one more time to make sure.

Proud eased his head around directly into a large hand that grabbed him by the hair and slammed his head into the wall. He was then thrown against the bulkhead which brought the loss of consciousness, and he suffered many strikes and kicks before his life force was drained away.

"Pete, Pete, can you hear me?" shouted the Captain into his communicator. Suddenly, Proud's communicator came to life, but the only sounds were what seemed like curious grunts and sniffing. The background noise heard before when speaking with LT Proud was now gone. That portion of A Deck was quiet as the attackers had moved on; on toward the Bridge.

Captain Ward shouted to his Communications Officer, "Get a line to the Admiral! Now! Then send the computer logs for the last two hours to him."

"Aye Captain," replied a frightened Lieutenant JG Alicia Garcia.

It took but seconds for Admiral King to answer. "Yes, Al, what is happening?"

"Sir, we are under attack by cavemen or aliens. They are killing everyone they come across. It will only be seconds before they are upon us." Ward went on to describe the events leading up to his call to Admiral King.

Admiral King was about to ask for more information when Ward shouted, "They're here, abandon stations, fight or die!" The sounds of hand to hand combat filled the airwaves until, after only a very few minutes, the only sounds coming from Astrid were angry sounding grunts.

"JJ, initiate thirty-eight Protocol, now."

Yes, sir, done.

The survivors aboard the three mining ships felt the ship's engines suddenly surge to full thrust as thirty-eight Protocol kicked in.

Within a few days, the surviving cavemen were dying of thirst. By day five, there was no living thing aboard the Astrid, Phobos, or Deimos as they made their two-year voyage into the sun.

26 FEBRUARY 2118
ABOARD USSN LEYTE GULF
EN ROUTE TO EARTH

Admiral King was deeply affected by the plight and final disposition of his ships. He was especially saddened by the loss of his friend Captain Alan Ward.

"JJ, patch me into Admiral Perry."

Yes, sir, he is ready.

"Dolph, were you listening to the dying moments of the Astrid?"

"Good," said King, "I don't relish repeating those events. Sir, I ordered thirty-eight Protocol to be put into effect, but I would like for Captain Ward to get the credit for that order. He died a hero, and I would like for him to be remembered for his sacrifices. JJ, tap into the uploaded computer logs from the Astrid and forward them to Admiral Perry."

Yes, sir will do.

"Sir," said Sky King, the Earth is about to be force-fed a huge crap sandwich. I'll be waiting for your orders."

Dolph said, "Yes, I'm afraid we are. I'll get back to you immediately following the upcoming meeting with President Greene. Are you okay, Sky?"

"No, I am not, but yes, I will be. I hope you understand. Sir, please get all of our Spacers and their families onto transports and headed to Mars. I have a feeling that Man's future lies there. Admiral, get yourself on one of those transports. You will be needed on Mars."

The Vice-Admiral hesitated before saying, "I don't know, Sky, I'll speak to the Prez about it. Dolph: Out."

26 FEBRUARY 2118, 1900 HOURS
PRESIDENT'S CONFERENCE ROOM
WHITE HOUSE
WASHINGTON, DC, USA

Admiral Perry met with his President before the meeting and gave her the bad news. Once everyone was seated the President directed Admiral Perry to brief the Comet Committee on the events aboard the Astrid and her sister ships.

"Madame President, as reported to this committee on 7 February, the hulls of all three of the mining vessels were holed from the debris storm which was the result of the SRI-F nuclear attack on Holly Thorne. Each ship performed a quick series of EVA missions to make temporary repairs to the hulls. The missions were completed, but unfortunately, over three-hundred crewmen were lost, including two crewmen on EVA repair tasks were also lost into the maelstrom.

"The forty remaining crewmen on EVA tasks reentered their ships. At this point, the mission was completed, and the three ships began the voyage back to Mars. Admiral King, then informed both Red Sands and NASA that they were ending the mission and the mining vessels had set course to return to the Mars facilities for repair and refit.

"All communications remained normal, until the morning of 8 February. Red Sands received a message from Captain Flynn, Commanding the USSN Leyte Gulf. She stated that crew members from all three of the mining ships had become infected with a virulent strain of something with extreme flu-like symptoms.

"Red Sands Control then informed Captain Flynn that these ships will not be allowed to dock with the Space Station until the medical emergency was ended. Once the flu had run its course, a medical team would be dispatched to evaluate the situation.

"On 18 February, Captain Ward agreed. He also informed Admiral King that Captains Putin and Chen had not survived the epidemic. The three Mining Vessels will continue to a position beyond Mars and await the medical teams from Red Sands.

"Admiral King's vessels, enroute to Earth, reports that no one on the seven SDF ships has become ill. The SDF would continue to Earth and await further orders. Their anticipated arrival date is 21 March 2118.

"Now, here is where the really bizarre part comes in. On 22 February Captain Ward reported that nearly fifty percent of his surviving crew members were nowhere to be found. They had apparently gone into hiding and would not report for duty. The Captain attempted to find these errant spacers, but they were so well hidden that their whereabouts remained unknown."

The President interrupted, saying, "Why would half of the surviving crew go into hiding?"

"Madame President," said Gordon, "at that point, the Captain had no idea what had caused this phenomenon. Four days later, on 26 February, the Captain alerted Admiral King, aboard the Leyte Gulf, that a mutiny was occurring on each vessel."

"A mutiny?" asked the President.

"Yes, ma'am, but not a mutiny in the historical lexicon. The Captain's last words came as he and his Bridge Crew were fighting for their lives. He shouted that Cavemen were attacking and killing the crew. In his final communication, many loud grunts could be heard as the fight raged on the bridge. His final act was to go to full thrust and alter course thirty-eight degrees from the ecliptic and out of the Solar System."

CDC asked to speak.

"Yes, please," said the President, "I hope you can shed some light on this."

"Madame President, at this point I only have questions. Admiral, you said Cavemen?"

"That is what Captain Ward reported, He said, Cavemen with square heads, low brows, and squared eye sockets. The recording contains several, aggressive sounding grunts and angry roars, along with the shouts of the Bridge Crew. We can only assume that upon assuming command of the Astrid, Captain Ward had been brought in on the utilization of the Thirty-Eight Protocol and that he initiated it. The three vessels then turned, as one, changing course to thirty-eight degrees from the ecliptic and going to full thrust. Captain Ward was a very brave man."

General Howard asked, "Well, by making the move at thirty-eight degrees from the ecliptic we know that he did, indeed, initiate the protocol. In two years, those ships will dive into the sun."

NASA said, "The Captain had only a few moments to contemplate this move, so it must have been put into action quickly. Our people are searching for answers as to what they were facing."

"Tyler," asked the President, "can we be sure this flu came from Holly Thorne?"

"At this moment, Madame President, I can only offer a supposition, no wait, no more disclaimers. Yes, I believe it gained entry into the spacecraft via the hull breaches. The remaining seven vessels of Taffy III have not been affected by any illness. This certainly gives us one additional bit of evidence that the infection resulted from the hull breaches.

"In 1918, just following the 1st World War, the flu epidemic, later named the Spanish Flu (H1N1) erupted in a worldwide pandemic that took as many as one-hundred million lives.

"Now, the name Spanish Flu is a misnomer, because this pandemic did not start in Spain. Instead, it began all over the world at the same time. No medical researcher has ever been able to explain how this could happen, perhaps today, but not in 1918. Of note, here, is that just before that outbreak the Earth passed through the tail of a comet, so yes ma'am, I believe Holly Thorne is the only viable suspect at this point."

Eileen steepled her fingers under her chin, tapping the index fingers together as she sat for several seconds in deep thought. Raising her head, she asked, "Gordon, you say we'll spend four days passing through the tail of Holly Thorne?"

"Yes, ma'am, and if CDC is correct, we could be, well, we, we could be facing an Extinction Level Event, an E.L.E. If that virus came through the holes in the ship's hulls, then we will become infected as we pass through the comet's tail."

General Howard said, "I don't see how that is possible, even if half of our population does turn into Zombies…"

"Sorry, General, but the term used by Captain Ward was Cavemen, not Zombies. If these Cavemen were our latest ancestral cousin, they are known to us as Cro-Magnon Man."

Frustrated, General Howard said, "Toe may-toe, toe-mah-toe, our military can handle a bunch of Cro-Magnon Cave dwellers."

Tyler, from CDC, said, "Okay, let's talk this through. Captain King said that 100% of his crews were infected and that 75% died; that's eight-thousand dead on each ship. Of the survivors, 50% turned into these Cavemen. Let's give them a name, I suggest Mags, as in Cro-Magnon.

"So, if 75% of the Earth's population dies, and 50% of the survivors become Mags, then we have a healthy population of 12.5%. The deaths of 75% of the human population will, at the very least, end modern civilization as we know and understand it. Add to this that one-half of the surviving population intends to kill us, I have to think that even if modern Man can defeat the Mags, our nation will not survive, no nation will survive. General, I suppose that you could be right, this may, or may not, be an E.L.E. but it will still bring civilization crashing down around us."

General Howard snorted as he added, "Harrumph, our modern weapons in the hands of the surviving military will make minced meat of these Mags."

President Greene said, "General if your military is drawn down to only 12.5% of current strength, I wonder how they will do in the first moments of being attacked by Mags? The military will not have weapons.

"I also wonder how we will feed your remaining military? How will we feed one-hundred thousand troops scattered all over the country when the distribution of food, hell, distribution of everything just stops? Tyler, you were rather specific about defining these Mags as Cro-Magnon. What led you to that conclusion?" asked President Greene.

"Yes, of course, Madame President, considering the minimal information of this disease and its after-effects what I am about to say is pure speculation. I do, however, believe that it may have merit. I suspect this is the case from the description, specifically of the squared eye sockets.

"It would seem that we have a disease which, in fifty percent of the survivors, alters the human appearance down to the molecular level. This would explain why the soon to be Mags went into hiding four days after their recovery. Their time in hiding allowed the transformation to take place without hindrance from any medical person, or their shipmates.

"I use the term Cro-Magnon because they are our nearest relative on the evolutionary path to us. Cro-Magnon Man remains were first found in France. The property owner was named Magnon, and so the remains became Cro-Magnon.

"Research on these modern humans indicates that they arrived in Western Europe around forty-thousand years ago. They invaded the lands which had been occupied by a group called the Neanderthal, for nearly one-hundred-thousand years. Many researchers believe that Cro-Magnon Man was one of the critical factors in the elimination of the Neanderthal.

"I, therefore, have really gone out on a limb and have hypothesized that as an invader, the Mags, were aggressive. Mags stood around five feet ten inches in height, with a low brow and a somewhat square head, even their eye sockets were squared. They were heavily built, very strong and, we believe, very fast. This description, especially of square eye sockets is the guiding factor in my recommendation to call them Mags.

"They were thinkers and inventors that primarily hunted large game, like Mammoths, Cave Bears and the like. To level the playing ground with their larger and stronger prey, Mags invented the spear thrower…"

"Spear thrower!" said a scornful General Howard, "Spear thrower, and you wonder if even a small modern military force would have difficulty in destroying them? Please!"

Tyler looked at Howard and said, "General, these spear throwers could launch spears at speeds approaching ninety miles per hour. These spear throwers you so casually dismiss took down Mammoths, Cave Bears, and Lions that stood taller than you at the shoulder.

"Tactically, you are right, Mags would have no chance against a well-armed military, but, sir, these Mags will not all be facing your soldiers, they will be spread all over the hemisphere, and it is likely that they will quickly begin to eliminate competition… us. I fully realize that the US has a plethora of weapons available to the populace, but in the initial stages of this war to come, the Mags will strike before Man can become organized to fight them.

"As soon as the Mags come out of hiding, they will come out to fight, and to make matters even worse, we can't warn the survivors of the coming of the Mags and their potentially primal urge to eliminate all competition.

"The initial arrival of Mags could number as many as forty-five million, and they will all arrive at about the same time. If we extrapolate what we heard from the Astrid broadcasts, the Mags will come out swinging for the fences."

General Howard looked back at CDC and said, "Oh, shit! Oh, sorry Madame President. I apologize for my language."

President Greene's face was pale as she looked back at the general as she said, "You took the words right out of my mouth. Oh shit, indeed."

Then turning back to Tyler, she said, "Tyler, I do not like this scenario. Is there anything the CDC can do? Can we begin an inoculation program for flu shots?"

"Madame President," said Tyler, "We have neither a serum prepared, nor even an earnest idea whether this bug really is a flu strain, and we can't even begin to look for a cure until the virus strikes so that we have a sample.

"With your permission, ma'am, I will immediately call in the entire CDC, along with the Fort Detrick folks and secure them in our upgraded level 5 labs. If we are very lucky, these researchers will remain uninfected and can begin working on a cure the moment people begin to get sick.

"But, Madame President, this is probably just pie in the sky, but it is the only option that I can imagine at this point."

"Why is your suggestion pie in the sky, Tyler?" asked Eileen.

Tyler produced a somewhat sick smile, and said, "Because everyone will get sick at the same time, and by the time we get started, well, this plan has so many holes, but it is the only plan we have. I would also suggest that no later than 3 March you take the Rangers into the continuity of government bunkers. You'll also need to take in their families."

"All right, Tyler, but what do we do for the people of our nation? There must be something?"

The Chief of Staff lowered his head and in a low, sad voice, hardly above a whisper said, "It's too late, isn't it?"

No one spoke as the realization that, it was, in point of fact, too late, and to make this horror story public would only bring on additional tragedy on a global scale. The veneer of civilization would immediately be stripped away. The moral shackles of civility would be gone in an instant. No, just pretend that all is well and let the chips fall where they may.

General Howard finally said, "Madame President, you will be moving to the Mount Weather Facility on 3 March."

Ladies and Gentlemen," said General Triple H Howard, "I give each of you fair warning that I swear before the Lord God Jehovah that I will personally shoot anyone who leaks this info. Are we clear? No leaks, not to anyone, no exceptions. If you think I am just being overly dramatic, you are sadly mistaken. Speak about this, and you will die."

President Greene said, "Congress, General?"

"Especially the Legislative Branch, ma'am, to have even a remote possibility of saving something of our Republic, you must not bring Congress or the Senate in. When the opportunity arises, you must rule, with only your VPOTUS. There will be no survival if the Legislative Branch continues its bickering and inaction. Besides, there will be no states remaining for them to represent."

"Triple H, put your plan into operation. We'll put it out that everyone is being called in to study the tail's impact on our atmosphere and the debris fields."

Admiral Perry asked to speak, "Madame President, I understand that cold fusion has not, to this point, created any dangerous side effects, such as radiation. Yet, I must, in the strongest terms possible submit that we must immediately begin shutting down all cold fusion power plants. With your permission, I will order the immediate shutdown of all cold fusion powered vessels, with the exception of our submarine forces. I will direct them to find deep water and bottom their boats. Once the crap hits the proverbial fan, they will be notified to remain submerged for a minimum of two years. All of our subs are provisioned up to four years. Hopefully, by that time the strain will have died out, and our submarine service will be able to assist in recovery efforts.

"Our Space Defense Force will begin the immediate transition, with families, to Red Sands. I suggest we tell the media that we are planning deep space exercises lasting for up to two years. This will explain why we are taking the spacer's families."

"Good thinking, Admiral, make it happen. My friends, we have one week to get the preparations completed, and those selected will depart at times allowing for arrival no later than two hours before Holly Thorne's tail bites us in the ass."

Almost as an afterthought, President Greene asked for both her Chief of Staff and Admiral Perry to remain after the meeting." Before the meeting, Greene and the COS discussed a new role for Vice Admiral Perry.

With the other Comet Committee members gone, Eileen said, "Dolph, I have a special mission for you."

"Yes, ma'am, of course. How may I be of assistance?"

"Dolph, you will not be accompanying me to Mount Weather. Instead, I am reassigning you as the Supreme Commander of the Red Sands, Mars USSDF Headquarters. You are also promoted to the five-star rank of Fleet Admiral. My friend, I am terribly sorry that this promotion could not be a grand occasion, but I'm sure you realize that is not possible.

"You will also carry with you documents which will grant complete nationhood to Red Sands. You will also turn over all of the USSDF vessels to the new government on Mars. Please do not release these documents until we are sure that the Earth does indeed fall into complete anarchy.

"You are also being entrusted with the original, and several copies of the Constitution. It is my hope that Red Sands will find them useful. There are a number of other things to be sent with you for safe keeping.

"You and your immediate staff will be taken to the Washington Space Elevator for transit to our Space Station. There you will assume command of the transport vessels. Coordinate with Admiral King to a rendezvous where you are to assume overall command of Taffy III. The three remaining Cruisers will follow on 5 March to join you on Mars. You must also integrate any and all space going vessels, from whatever nation.

"Dolph, I will miss you, and I wish you well. You must succeed. Failure is not an option. Are we clear?"

"Yes, Madame President," said a sad and suddenly weary Fleet Admiral Adolphus Perry. "When should I plan to leave?"

The Chief of Staff said, "Dolph, go home, pack your necessary items and get you and your family to the Elevator. Your staff is being rounded up as we speak. Time is of the essence, my friend." The President and her COS began standing. Once all three were on their feet, the COS shook hands with the first Fleet Admiral since 1946. President Eileen N. Greene gave Dolph a hug and a kiss on the cheek for luck. Goodbyes were completed, and Dolph was driven to his quarters.

On the ride home, Dolph and Sky, using their AIs, discussed the meeting and before Sky could ask, Dolph told him that Hermie would see him soon.

Sky said, "Well, Fleet Admiral, you, my friend, have your work cut out for you. How may I help?"

"I am so glad you asked, Vice Admiral King, because we have our work cut out for us. Civilization must continue and one day return it to Earth," said Dolph.

For the next three days, preparations went well. The media bought the story of studying the atmospheric effects of Holly Thorne, and the transition of the SDF to Mars, along with their families.

27 FEBRUARY 2116, AD 1500
PALEONTOLOGY DEPARTMENT
WEST VIRGINIA UNIVERSITY
MORGANTOWN, WV

Thirty-eight-year-old Professor Jacob Abraham sat at his desk reviewing applications from students desirous of joining him on a newly approved dig in Moundsville, WV.

His expectation had been ten to twelve volunteers seeking experience in both archaeology and paleontology. Jakob's eyes ached from reviewing the twenty-eight applications now in front of him. Two of the apps were from Pitt, well, there were two he could reject. The rivalry between WVU and Pitt made for a mixture of gasoline and water

Once Professor Abraham had settled on interviewing twenty-seven applications for the twenty-two positions. Scheduling interviews for these eager beavers sounded simple. Simple, until class schedules of both Professorial and Student class loads inevitably threw a monkey wrench into the equation. Jake sent emails to each of the student volunteers chosen for an interview, then sat back and awaited their responses.

Jake was pleasantly surprised to see the results of his email. Within minutes the requests for interviews flooded his inbox. Even more surprising were the responses which indicated that they would come at the time specified by Professor Abraham. He quickly began sending interview times.

Jake felt a bit under the gun, as the dig was to begin on March 6, 2018. Everything else was ready, packed, and loaded on the eight pick-up trucks, along with one eight-passenger mini-bus, which he would drive.

As Jake was about to call it quits for the day, he heard a knock on his Office Door. "Come on in," he shouted at the door.

As the door opened Jake saw that it was the student he had selected for the paid position on his dig, Gale Storm. Jake didn't see her walk, to his eyes she swam into the room.

"Well, hello Miss Storm, did you receive my email?" Try as he might he could not take his eyes completely away from the exotic face of Gale Storm. There was nothing in the way of classic beauty in this self-assured, tall, lanky woman. Jake tried to come up with a description of what made her so attractive to him, and the only word that seemed to fit was exotic.

Professor Abraham had not once done more than admire a lovely student, but Gale Storm was different. Gale was somehow different, and Jake was smitten. *Shit,* thought Jake.

"Please, Miss Storm, have a seat."

"Thank you, sir, I did receive your email, and since I was in the building, I thought I would stop by before heading off to work."

Jake felt an immediate dismay, that wasn't entirely professional. "Oh, you already have a job. I see. Are you here to tell me that you won't be able to join the dig?" Jake hoped his disappointment wasn't betrayed by his voice or eyes.

Gale smiled and said, "No, sir, not a chance. I work part-time as a bartender at the Dog and Pony. A gal has gotta' eat, you know?"

"Yes, I do know," said Jake, I worked my way through my Ph.D., though I do admit that I was fortunate enough to be able to find Research Assistant's positions following my Master's Program. Before that, I worked as a server at a Texas Roadhouse Restaurant, and before you ask, yes, I hated it."

Both were now smiling and obviously enjoying each other's company when Jake asked, "Well, Miss Storm, with your experience on previous digs and the references I got from the Team Leaders, I am pleased to offer your first paying Paleontology gig. Are you in?"

"Oh hell, yes," blurted out an immediately embarrassed Gale. "I'm sorry, sir, that just slipped out. What I meant to say was, yes sir, I would be honored to accept your offer of employment."

Jake chuckled and said, "Oh hell, yes, you're hired. Can you be ready to leave in six days?"

"Yes, sir, that's no problem, I've already told the owner that I might be leaving for this job. He wasn't crazy about any short notices, but he understood and wished me well. So, yes indeed, what time do you want me to be here and ready to travel?"

"March 5th at 8:00 a.m. What's your class load for the rest of the semester?"

"I only have two classes to finish up my Master's Degree. I have already spoken with the instructors about the possibility that I might get this job, and they have agreed to let me go. Lucky me, I don't have any more classes this week, so I guess I'm all done."

Jake smiled again and said, "Gale, that is wonderful news. You are on the clock beginning tomorrow morning at 8:00 a.m. You will be interviewing several of the applicants. We have room for twenty-one more positions to fill, and there are twenty-six applicants. My guess is that the extras will return emails saying that they are unable to go. A few will drop off the list. It happens every time. Experience in the interview process will serve you well in the future. You will sit in on four interviews beginning tomorrow morning and then you are on your own; any questions?"

"No, sir, no questions, and I thank you for this opportunity. I won't let you down."

"No, Miss Storm, I don't think you will. Your resume and references have made me very comfortable."

"Professor Abraham, please call me Gale."

"All right, Gale it is. If there is nothing else, I will see you in the morning at 8:00 sharp."

"Yes, sir," gushed Gale as she stood to leave.

Walking down the hallway she was so happy that she became short of breath causing the floor to sway under her feet.

7 days to Holly Thorne

27 FEBRUARY 2118
WSAZ TV NEWS
CHARLESTON, WV

An announcer identified the man sitting at the Anchor Desk of WSAZ's evening news as Todd Stone. "Good evening and welcome to the WSAZ six o'clock news, I'm Todd Stone and the big event in tonight's broadcast is the arrival of Comet Holly Thorne. We have just one more week until the big event. I know I'm excited. Holly is now visible even at noon. This is really going to be something, folks. Our meteorologist Summer Reign is on hand to tell us all about the coming light display. Summer?"

The camera switched from Stone to Summer; "thank you, Todd. Good evening everyone, I'm Summer Reign, Chief Meteorologist for your WSAZ primetime news.

"Wow, what a light-show we are going to have in just one more week. At precisely 9:05 pm on March 6th the Kanawha Valley will begin to see the incredible display of lights as we pass through the tail of Comet Holly Thorne. The show will continue for four days, and we will see this giant comet clearly, even at noon as it makes its grand passage toward the sun."

Summer turned to her sixty-inch wall screen which came alive showing the progress of the largest comet ever reported, live from the American Space Station, and the Lunar Colony.

Summer turned back to the camera and said, "The three asteroid mining freighters tasked to nudge this giant far enough outside the orbit of Luna, allowing the comet to safely slide past the Earth did an incredible job.

"Our planet will sail through a portion of Holly Thorne's tail for approximately one-hundred-thousand miles before exiting this magnificent view of nature's artistic palette."

For several minutes Summer continued to point out important expectations of what was being called The Greatest Show on Earth.

"I'm so excited," said Summer. "This will not happen again in our lifetime, so don't miss out. Back to you, Todd."

"Thank you, Summer, I know I'm looking forward to sitting out on the lawn with family and friends to watch the fireworks."

Todd dramatically turned his chair from the network Weather Station to face the camera before his desk. "We have just received some rather sad news from NASA and our Space Force.

"It appears that approximately ten days following a space-walk mission to repair several hull breaches to the mining ships from the comet's debris, according to a joint statement from NASA and our Space Defense Force, communications have been lost with all three ships. NASA fears that the hull breaches have resulted in the loss of these true heroes. Their fate is, at this point, unknown. Our thoughts and prayers are with those brave souls.

2 MARCH 2118
USSN FLOTILLA
USSDF SPACE STATION

A twenty-two-ship flotilla, consisting of five rented Cruise Ships, five civilian freighters, six USSDF Container Ships, and the last three SDF Cruisers in orbit around the Earth formed up and departed the homeworld bound for Mars. The USSDF Space Station was placed in tow by two SDF Tugs. The flotilla would meet up with the seven SDF Cruisers of Taffy III approximately half-way to Mars. This hodgepodge of space going vessels certainly did not have a military look, but it was civilizations last real hope.

The Container Ships carried huge amounts of material to assist in the Red Sands building plan. There were nearly one-thousand cold fusion reactors that would be dedicated to the terraforming of Mars. These additional reactors would make Mars habitable in only fifty more years.

Once emptied, the Container Ships would be converted to orbiting Green Houses.

Red Sands was about to have a population explosion.

2 MARCH 2118
MOUNT WEATHER

The Presidential Bunker at Mount Weather continued to receive the unending lines of Semi-Trucks which were supplying the bunkers.

Two Ranger Battalions were busy holding training exercises around Mount Weather.

Those additional staff members and families selected to occupy *the Continuity of Government Bunkers* would be alerted to prepare for transportation eight hours before their scheduled evacuations. They would be kept under guard to prevent contact with family and friends, while they packed.

It rapidly became apparent that the foresight of the members of the Holly Thorne Committee had proved to be prophetic.

By failing to alert the Legislature to the possible danger of the approaching comet, the News Networks remained calm, as it was obvious that the Legislative Branch did not appear to be making any special preparations.

Massive celebrations were being scheduled around the globe to party like it's 1999. World problems and old hatreds were seemingly forgotten as the human race embraced the coming stellar show. Everyone felt the excitement of Holly's approach.

2 MARCH 2118 9:00 PM
THE DOG AND PONY BAR
MOUNDSVILLE, WV

Jake tried hard to ignore his attraction to Gale, but it wasn't in the cards. He found himself sidling up to the bar at The Dog and Pony. She had wrangled a bar tender's gig to keep herself fed while on the dig.

Turning from the bottles behind the bar, she found herself looking at the man who, to her green eyes, was the real-life Indiana Jones, Jacob Abraham. He also had a fedora over his lush light brown hair, and like the movie version of Indiana Jones, Jake wore a leather jacket but preferred jeans and desert boots. He stood 5'10" tall, one inch shorter than Gale. She thought him to be quite handsome, but it was his disarming smile that made her heart skip a beat.

"Oh, hello, Professor Abraham," said Gale. "What can I getcha?"

Jake ordered a Dos Equis.

Of course, it would be a Dos Equis, thought Gale, *what else would the most interesting man in the world drink?* Without thinking she smiled at the thought.

"What?" asked Jake, "Did I say something funny?"

"Oh, no sir, not funny, exactly. I just had an errant thought is all."

Jake smiled back at her and asked, "A penny for your thought."

Embarrassed now, Gale stuttered out, "It's gone now, I don't even remember what it was."

Jake knew she was evading his question but felt that continuing to ask would not be in his best interests. Changing the subject, he said, "Tell me, Gale, how did your parents decide on such a great name?"

Gale appreciated his moving away from her thought of him drinking Dos Equis beer. She gave Jake a wry smile and said, "My parents were both Meteorologists. They thought that by naming me, Gale, I might follow in their footsteps. Uh, no, the name itself kept me from developing a taste for predicting the weather."

Without thinking, Jake said, "I'm glad, since it brought you to want to dig up old bones."

Not sure if Jake was using a double entendre, Gale said, "Excuse me, but I happen to like old bones; especially those that drink Dos Equis. Oh, I didn't mean that the way it came out, I am so sorry, Professor Abraham. I didn't mean to, oh, I don't know, now I'm just embarrassed."

Jake just smiled at her and said, "Gale, even though I am nearly ten years your elder, I am going to go out on a limb, here. Okay, here goes, Miss Storm, would you consider having dinner with an older man? That would be with me, of course."

Now Gale became a bit cautious, and she said, "Professor Abraham, you must know that I find you very attractive, but I'm not some young first-year star struck deb looking for an A by letting you into my pants. So, if that's what you are hoping for, my answer is no."

Jake sat his Dos Equis long neck down on the bar and said, "Miss Storm, I honestly had no such idea in mind. I hope you know that I do not have a reputation for chasing pretty students. In the five years of my teaching career, I have never before asked one of my students to join me for dinner, or for anything else.

"So, if you will excuse me, I will slink out of here before attempting to bandage my bruised ego and hope you can forgive my feeble attempt at asking you for a dinner date. Good evening, Miss Storm," said a most embarrassed Jake Abraham as he rose from his stool to leave.

"Wait," said an equally embarrassed Gale Storm, "Look, I won't be a Professor's trophy, so if you're not just looking for a one-night rodeo, then, yes, I would love to join you for dinner, but, why me? There are several real lookers on the team."

Sitting back down on his bar stool, Jake switched back from Miss Storm to Gale and said, "Gale, to say such a thing is to do an absolute disservice to yourself. It's true, there are some lovely young ladies on our dig team, but I'm here because I find you mesmerizing. I have never in my life asked a student for a date. Am I rambling?"

"Just a little," laughed Gale. Okay, when would you like to take me to dinner, before you try to sweep me off my feet?"

"Gale, are your disclaimers meant as a defensive tool, or are you just a wise ass?"

Both laughed, albeit a bit nervously before Gale said, "A little of both I guess; still want to give me a whirl?"

"Of course, so, when do you get off, from work, I mean."

"Oh, very clever Professor Wise Ass." Then turning she called out, "Wendell, would you call Adelle and ask if she can relieve me tonight?"

Wendell shouted back, "Sure, Gale, will do." He then picked up his phone and dialed Adelle.

After a moment, he shouted back, "Adelle says, sure, she'll be here in thirty minutes."

"Thanks, Wendell, you da man!"

Gale smiled at Jake and said, "What a coincidence, I just happen to be free this very evening."

3 MARCH 2118, 0300
MOUNT WEATHER

The President of the United States of America, the most powerful person in the world, was led by a Secret Service Detachment through one of the most secret tunnels exiting the White House. Electric golf carts ferried the President, The First Gentleman, and her primary staff to a nondescript building three blocks from the White House.

The party exited the building and entered a bus. The President and her husband Lamar were transported in a blue older model Chrysler Mini-Van.

There was no long parade of vehicles or police escorts. This trip was completely clandestine, and it went off without a hitch. Sitting in the second row of seats in the van, President Greene was despondent. She felt as though she was sneaking away from the oncoming danger, while leaving her fellow Americans to pay the piper. This was, of course, exactly what she was doing. The saving grace was the fervent hope that once the danger was over, she could return and with the personnel and material stored inside Mount Weather, get a head start on beginning the long road to re-establishing the nation.

At the same time, the Vice President was being whisked away to Cheyenne Mountain. The trip to Mount Weather took a bit over one hour. Upon her arrival a new and fragile government was formed; a benevolent dictatorship for the foreseeable future.

6 MARCH 2118
MOUNDSVILLE, WV

Jacob Abraham had just arrived at a newly opened archeology site near Moundsville, West Virginia. The site originated with an Indian culture called The Mound Builders. Though Jake was anxious to get started, his mind kept slipping to the upcoming Holly Thorne light show.

Jake's team of Archeology and Paleontology students were excited to finally be involved in an actual dig site. Gale Storm was Professor Abraham's Research Assistant and oversaw student assignments. She thought of it as a combination of Task Master and Den Mother.

She wasted no time in organizing her charges into work details to get the tents for living quarters and dining set up. The afternoon would be Jake's turn to organize the actual dig site and get his students to work. Once Jake's rah-rah and what we need to do speech was finished he turned the operation over to Gale.

Jake's job would be to keep a watchful eye on progress and see to the recovery and classification of any artifacts that he hoped would be recovered.

Jake had been smitten with Gale from the first instant of their meeting. She was tall, and lanky, with light auburn hair that reflected the sun's rays. Perhaps Gale's most alluring feature were her bright green eyes that somehow seemed to focus all attention her way. She was no Miss America, but she, none the less attracted more than her fair share of admiring glances. Gale took Jake's breath away. Now, after only four days since their first date, they had become lovers.

CHAPTER THIRTEEN

ZERO DAYS TO HOLLY THORNE

The Celebrations

MARCH 6, 2118
EARTH

"From the FOX News anchor desk in New York City, here is Sheldon Smith," said the voice over.

"Good afternoon everyone, I'm Sheldon Smith, well, it's just a little more than two hours until the party of the century officially kicks off. Though I must say that from the looks of the crowds around the world, the party is already in full swing.

"On this day, March 6, 2118, the nations of this world seem to have put their grievances aside to welcome this once in many lifetimes event. The last time the Earth passed through the tail of a comet was in 1918, that's two hundred years ago, folks.

"In New York City's Times Square, New Orleans French Quarter, Rio, Paris, Munich, Amsterdam, and hundreds of other cities the hysteria for the Holly Thorne Comet is reaching a fever pitch.

"Our planet will enter the tail of Holly Thorne with New York's street party leading the way. At exactly 9:47 pm the cosmic fireworks begin, and NASA assures us that we will never forget the light show that is coming this way in just another two hours and fifty-one minutes.

"NASA has also issued the warning that an occasional bit of Holly Thorne may be large enough to reach the ground. So, keep an eye out for the souvenir that could make you rich.

"The security forces are already highly visible and proactive, to deter fights and riots. We take you first to a Live stream from FOX News: Mel Capp."

"Thanks, Sheldon, well folks, today marks the beginning of mass celebrations across the globe. The skies over New York are blue and cloudless, temperatures are hovering in the mid-fifties. There's also a five mile per hour breeze pushing through the steel-sided canyons of The Big Apple.

"Here, in Times Square, the crowd numbers match those of New Year's Eve, with much better weather. If you want to party this night, then Times Square is the place to be. Back to you, Sheldon."

"Thank you, Mel. Next, we have FOX Entertainment News: Correspondent Gavin Coates reporting from Rio. Gavin, what is the mood in Rio?"

"Good evening Shel, here in Rio the city is a madhouse of ecstatic partiers. The streets are overflowing with revelers, parades, and, of course, thousands of beautiful, scantily clad ladies everywhere you look. As you know, Rio is in the same time zone as New York, and there must already be two-million partiers in the streets."

Similar coverage continued from sites around the world.

Not everyone, however, took to the streets. Millions across the globe chose to ride out the first night of Earth's passage through Holly

Thorne's tail, in shelters as the possibility of the comet's debris crashing through the atmosphere.

MARCH 6, 2118
MOUNT WEATHER
PRESIDENTIAL BUNKER

Angry and confused families of Service Members were hustled to the Mount Weather and Cheyenne Mountain underground cities. Most of those angry at being brought into Mount Weather felt that they should have been able to contact family and friends to let them know where they would be.

Some of the confused joined the angry group, but many began to suspicion that the appearance of Holly Thorne might not turn out to be the party of the century, after all.

The Ranger Battalions were safely ensconced in the bunker and were joined with their families. Married soldiers were provided quarters with a modicum of privacy, while single men and women were placed in dormitories.

At 1600 hours on 6 March 2118, the bunkers were sealed by the closing of the huge blast doors. Once the doors were sealed, they would not be reopened for an estimated two years.

The first evening meal was served at 1700 hours and was followed by a Town Hall type meeting from President Eileen N. Greene, which was broadcast throughout both the Mount Weather and Cheyenne Mountain communications systems.

"My fellow Americans," began President Greene, "I know that most of you are either angry or confused as to why you are here. I certainly understand why you are feeling these emotions. Everyone has received a packet which details the immediate future, though I will tell you now.

"As you all know, the comet named Holly Thorne will pass the Earth by a wide margin, thanks to the brave men and women of the Space Defense Force. These Spacers, using large laser arrays, were able to nudge this giant comet safely away from the orbits of Earth and Luna.

"This magnificent mission was entirely successful, but after completion of Operation HT, on February 1st, the Space Forces of the Sino-Russian-Indian Federation attacked both the comet and our fleet, named Taffy III.

"The attack led to the destruction of the entire SRI-F Fleet. However, one nuclear-tipped missile got through to Holly Thorne. This caused a large portion of debris to be cast off. Unfortunately, the missile blast sent pieces, which were ripped from the comet directly at the three mining vessels.

"They had no time to flee from the impacts from these small meteors and suffered many hits. All three vessels were damaged, but the crews were able to patch the holes in the ship's armor plating.

"Within hours these three ships began returning to the Red Sands Colony on Mars. Captain Alan Ward of the Astrid reported that over three-hundred souls were lost as a result of the damage from the comet.

"Each of these giant mining vessels carried a crew of twelve-thousand Spacers. Eight days later, on February 8th, Captain Ward reported that 100% of the crews had become extremely ill. He reported terrible flulike symptoms. The ships were all placed on auto-pilot, and the ill were sent to their quarters to recuperate.

"This inter-ship pandemic lasted for ten days. At that point, Captain Ward informed Admiral King that the death toll appeared to be roughly

75% of the crew. Each of these three ships lost roughly eight-thousand Spacers. The next four days were spent in cleanup operations to remove the dead to storage bays and kept at zero degrees Fahrenheit.

"On that fourth day, February 12th, Captain Ward again contacted Admiral King and informed him that approximately 50% of the surviving crew members had gone into hiding. As these ships are over three kilometers long the remaining Spacers were unable to find any of the absent personnel.

"This all changed on February 16th when those missing crew members came out of hiding. Now, here is the truly unimaginable portion of this saga. Those crewmen were no longer human. They had, over those four days, devolved into our most recent evolutionary cousin. They had all become a sub-species of Homo-Sapiens called Cro-Magnon. They immediately attacked and killed anyone they came across, finally eliminating the unarmed human crew.

"Captain Ward's last act, before his own death, was to initiate a computer program named Thirty-Eight Protocol which took all three ships out of the Solar System onto a course which will, in two years, fly into the sun.

"Unfortunately, this magnificent sacrifice will not prevent this pandemic from striking our planet. The tail of Holly Thorne contains a virus that we will not be able to avoid.

"Civilization, as we knew it, will disappear completely in the next twenty-six days. You have all been brought here to preserve a tiny portion of that civilization.

"I know how each of you must feel at this moment, as the realization that your extended families will soon become ill, and many will devolve into Cro-Magnons, which we have renamed as Mags. If we could have brought your families into the safety we have here, we most certainly would have, but there is simply insufficient space or supplies to accommodate them. I pray that you will soon see the necessity for these actions.

"There will be other communications in this format to both keep you informed on the progress of the disease, and the jobs that everyone will be required to do. Ultimately, it comes down to our being happy that we were all selected to survive and restart civilization. Good night, and may God bless and keep us all safe."

6 MARCH 2118
ARCHAEOLOGY DIG SITE
MOUNDSVILLE, WV

Holly Thorne was now huge in the night sky with a tail that seemed to stretch into infinity. Once the night overcame the fading rays of the sun, a light show like none any human had ever been privy to, streaked across the darkened sky.

The night had grown cool, but not uncomfortably so. Jacob Abraham and Gale Storm sat on folding lawn chairs, holding hands. They sat and watched the greatest show in the history of Man. The other team members had also paired off and were on blankets looking up at the thousands of shooting stars that were streaking across the sky.

Aborigines from the Rain Forests of South America, Micronesia, and elsewhere, reacted with dread. The coming of Holly Thorne had been unknown to them. In their hearts, they knew this event signaled the end of the world.

Inevitably, there were several meteors which struck the Earth's surface or exploded just before impact. None of these meteorites impacted any living person. Their remnants lay upon the Earth in many places, including both polar regions.

As the billions of people across the globe sat mesmerized by the spectacle before them, an unseen living microscopic organism rapidly covered the Planet Earth where this unknown virus found hosts in everyone not secured by virus proof facilities.

Those few who chose to seek shelter in basements did not become infected until they left their homes. The Earth was now a hothouse for a new and deadly virus that spared no one.

7 MARCH 2118
PRESIDENT GREENE
MOUNT WEATHER

After consultation with the Comet Committee, the consensus was that President Greene should address the nation.

"My fellow Americans, I am sorry to say to you that the CDC has detected a new and possibly serious virus which seems to have suddenly appeared everywhere around the world.

"The CDC has recommended that over the next few days everyone should stock up on sufficient foodstuffs to last for two-weeks. The CDC suggests that the foods you purchase should be those that are easily eaten and digested, like bread, jello, and pudding. They also suggest that you stock up on painkillers, such as Tylenol and large doses of vitamins, especially vitamin C. The Head of the CDC, Doctor Tyler Deen also recommends anti-diarrheal and anti-vomiting meds.

"At this point, it is unknown if the preparations will actually be needed, but it is better to have these items and not need them. Should you become ill with flu-like symptoms, do not plan on going to the hospital, or your family Doctor, as they may also be incapacitated.

"My friends, I would prefer that this warning was not needed, but the CDC believes that this new virus has been brought to us by the comet Holly Thorne.

"Please, I urge you not to panic. Don't purchase more of the recommended supplies than you will need for your families. If we remain calm, then things may well return to normal after ten days, or so. Remember, if you hoard, others may die as a result of your personal greed."

7 MARCH 2118
NEWS MEDIA
AROUND THE WORLD

The News Media went berserk with their coverage. CNN and their sister networks portrayed a nation in crisis. Though their coverage was inflammatory and caused horrendous panic buying, they were actually right about our nation and the world being in a new and deadly pandemic. According to them, the Spanish Flu was about to, again, rear its ugly head.

One ribbon ran across the Christian and Jewish News Networks that read, "Repent! The end is near."

While FOX News called for calm and encouraged their listeners to heed the President's words. Remain calm, don't panic, and don't hoard the CDC recommended supplies. Al Jazeera declared that the comet was bringing the 12th Imam. They celebrated the coming chaos.

Within hours of this outpouring of news, members of the government began showing up at every governmental bunker they could reach.

7 MARCH 2118
MOUNT WEATHER

Outside of the Mount Weather facility, hundreds of members of the Legislative Branch began showing up and demanding entrance.

A young Second Lieutenant, Calvin Dudley was the Duty Officer on 7 March 2118. He reported to the Chief of Staff that many people with children were gathering outside the complex wanting to be let in.

"Sir," said the Duty Officer, there are women and children out there. Should we open the door and let them in? Maybe they haven't become infected, yet?"

The COS responded with, "Lieutenant, if we open that door, we all die. I know this is heartrending and seems horribly selfish, but that door will not be opened. I want you to turn off the video and audio systems. There is to be no communication with anyone outside this facility. Are we clear on this?"

The young Second Lieutenant Dudley was not happy, but he said, "Yes, sir, we are clear."

"Good," said the COS, "now, I want to watch as you turn off the audio and video to the outside world."

With that, Mount Weather went dark.

Second Lieutenant Dudley, however, could not get the images of the children just outside the door out of his mind. Ten hours later, at 0200 hours, he turned the audio and video back on. Again, his heart began breaking. Dudley decided that denying them entrance to the bunker was tantamount to the murder of innocent women and children. At 0300 hours, he drew his sidearm and walked to the giant blast door.

When he came to within four feet of the Specialist (E-4) on guard duty, a wild-eyed, Lieutenant Dudley raised his pistol and told the guard that he was going to allow the women and children that were just on the other side of that door into Mount Weather.

Specialist Mathers looked down the barrel of the 9 mm service pistol and felt true fear. He could see the sadness or possibly madness in the eyes of this Lieutenant He said, "Sir, please put down your sidearm. I have been ordered to keep this door locked. If I open it, we will all die."

"Specialist," said Dudley, "if you don't open it, you will surely die right now. I cannot be a part of the murder of innocent women and their little children. Now, open the door!"

"Sir," said Mathers, "please, don't shoot. You must understand that the virus is out there, and even opening the door a crack will doom us all."

"You don't know that! You don't fucking know that, at all! What we do know is that if we don't open the door, those people outside will absolutely die. I cannot be a participant in the murder of children. Now, open that fucking door!"

"Lieutenant, I will not open the door. I can't, I have my orders from the President."

At this point Specialist Mathers lunged at Second Lieutenant Dudley in an attempt to take the sidearm. In the short struggle which ensued, Specialist Mathers was shot in the abdomen.

Moving quickly to get the door open before the shot brought the guard reaction force, Lieutenant Dudley pushed the lever which engaged the door. He allowed it to open only eighteen inches and shouted for the children to be put through.

Five young children made it through the door before the reaction force arrived and as Dudley turned to fire at the reinforcements, he was killed in a hail of gunfire.

The reaction force immediately shut the door and called the Officer of the Guard, who sent word up the line of the incident.

Three weeks later the only survivors in Mount Weather were two Secret Service Officers, and two-hundred and thirty-four Rangers. The highest-ranking surviving member of the military was a Corporal.

Second Lieutenant Dudley had done what he had hoped to prevent; the murder of thousands.

Once exposed to this Super-flu, survivors were immune from reinfection. With thousands of dead in Mount Weather, the Senior Secret Service Officer ordered the blast door opened to remove the bodies.

Two members of the Comet Committee survived the flu, and both turned. President Greene and her Chief of Staff were unrecognizable. They were buried along with the others in a mass grave.

15 MARCH 2118
PLANET EARTH

The morning of 15 March brought chaos and worldwide sickness. The entire world came under the spell of this devil virus between 14 and 15 March. No Hospitals were open as the medical staffs were ill and therefore unable to assist other sufferers.

For ten days everything across the world closed down as there were none strong enough to enable them to leave their residences. Billions died from the flu, starvation, and dehydration.

In ten days, the human population of the entire Earth fell to less than two-billion survivors. Four days later, on 19 March 2118, nearly one-billion survivors went into hiding.On 24 March, the Mags came out of hiding, and they came out swinging for the fences.

THE END

TO BE CONTINUED IN *THE OORT PLAGUE*

Cliff Deane grew up in South Charleston, West Virginia. At 17, he left school and joined the U.S. Cavalry, as a Private. 35 years later, he retired as a Lt. Colonel, spending 10 years Enlisted, and 25 years Commissioned.

Cliff holds a High School G.E.D., a Bachelor of Science Degree in Elementary Education and English, a Master's Degree in Education Administration and Management from West Virginia and is a graduate of the U.S. Army Command & General Staff College.

After retirement, a love of the American West took Cliff to Prescott, Arizona, which he has called home for many years.

Today, Cliff and his dog Katie reside full time in his 44' Toy Hauler. He and Katie just go where the wind blows, as long as the wind blows them to Sturgis, SD in August.

THANK YOU FOR READING!

If you enjoyed this book, we would appreciate your customer review on your book seller's website or on Goodreads.

Also, we would like for you to know that you can find more great books like this one at www.CreativeTexts.com

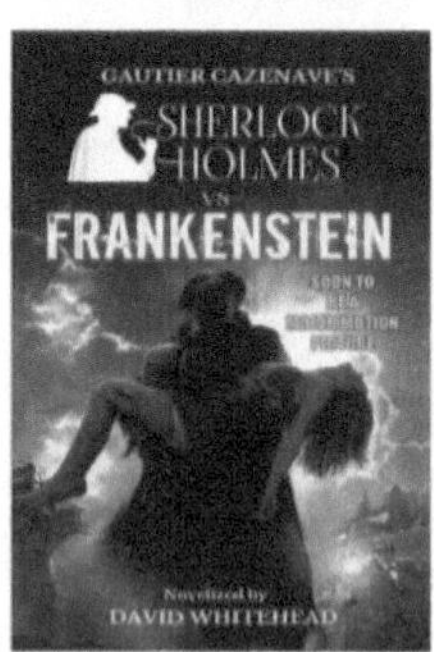

www.ingramcontent.com/pod-product-compliance
Lightning Source LLC
Chambersburg PA
CBHW030738110726
47900CB00008B/2356